HE SHOULD HAVE LOOKED OUT OF PLACE, BUT instead he seemed at ease with the wild elements, as if he had faced many a storm and survived. That quality could have been what had attracted her attention, she thought, because it was a quality she understood.

Idly she speculated about the color of his eyes. Black, perhaps, to go with his dark hair. Maybe blue. Or . . .

Suddenly he turned his head and looked at her, and she was almost knocked off her feet by the answer to her question. *Green.* His eyes were so dark a green, they seemed to hold the approaching storm.

And his hair—a slash of silver streaked through his dark hair, starting at the right side of his forehead and running straight back. Extraordinary . . .

All at once, in a blur of motion, he was there next to her and she felt an iron arm around her, trapping her. She tried to scream, but a white cloth covered her nose and mouth and then she was breathing in a sickly-sweet odor.

All these years she'd been ready for something like this to happen, and then she'd gone and let herself be knocked off guard by a pair of green eyes.

WHAT ARE *LOVESWEPT* ROMANCES?

They are stories of true romance and touching emotion. We believe those two very important ingredients are constants in our highly sensual and very believable stories in the LOVESWEPT *line. Our goal is to give you, the reader, stories of consistently high quality that may sometimes make you laugh, sometimes make you cry, but are always fresh and creative and contain many delightful surprises within their pages.*

Most romance fans read an enormous number of books. Those they truly love, they keep. Others may be traded with friends and soon forgotten. We hope that each LOVESWEPT *romance will be a treasure—a "keeper." We will always try to publish*

LOVE STORIES YOU'LL NEVER FORGET BY AUTHORS YOU'LL ALWAYS REMEMBER

The Editors

The Damaron Mark:
THE SINNER

FAYRENE PRESTON

BANTAM BOOKS
NEW YORK · TORONTO · LONDON · SYDNEY · AUCKLAND

THE DAMARON MARK: THE SINNER
A Bantam Book / August 1996

ISBN 0-553-44531-6

Published simultaneously in the United States and Canada

Bantam Books are published by Bantam Books, a division of Bantam Dou-
bleday Dell Publishing Group, Inc. Its trademark, consisting of the words
"Bantam Books" and the portrayal of a rooster, is Registered in U.S.
Patent and Trademark Office and in other countries. Marca Registrada.
Bantam Books, 1540 Broadway, New York, New York 10036.

PRINTED IN THE UNITED STATES OF AMERICA

OPM   0 9 8 7 6 5 4 3 2 1

ONE

One after another, the gray waves broke onto the rugged beach, creeping higher and higher up the rocky shore. The wind was sharp and cool and the lowering sun had long ago disappeared behind billowing dark clouds. The coming night was definitely not going to be an easy one.

Still, Jillian hated to leave. She loved this wild beach, situated along a craggy stretch of Maine coastline. Here, the winds and tides ruled, untamed. With the wind in her hair and the salt air on her skin, she found a sense of freedom. At this time of day, when the sun was setting and the few people who had ventured out earlier had gone home, the beach was irresistible to her. She was alone, just as she liked it.

But she was due at work in just over an

hour and she had to change. If the night proved too stormy, people might elect to eat at home rather than venture out to the restaurant where she waited tables, which meant Jimmy, the owner, would be in a good mood. She smiled to herself. Jimmy was the first restaurant owner she had met who was actually happiest when his place wasn't full. He didn't like to be too busy because he enjoyed the extra time to visit and gossip with his customers. She, on the other hand, was happiest when she was busy.

She pushed herself up from the boulder she'd been sitting on. Storm or no storm, a restaurant full or empty of patrons, she needed to be there. She considered herself lucky to have found the job six months ago, because she fit in so well. She worked while Jimmy visited.

As she began walking she saw him, a man, sitting on an outcropping of rocks, staring out at the churning sea. If she continued as she was going, she'd pass right by him.

She automatically stopped and tried to decide what to do. She could turn around and take a different path off the beach. Except . . .

She hesitated. There was something about him that made her want to study him.

His profile was toward her, and she received the distinct impression of power in repose. Set against the rugged landscape of the beach, he appeared in relief, his body lean, his face drawn with attractive lines, his coloring dark. He was wearing slacks, rather than the jeans most people favored for the rough beach, and an expensive-looking dark brown leather jacket. He should have looked out of place, but instead he seemed at ease with the wild elements, as if he had faced many a storm and survived. That quality could have been what had attracted her attention, she thought, because it was a quality she understood. Without further thought, she started along the path toward him, convinced he probably wouldn't even notice her.

Carefully she picked her way over the uneven ground. And as she drew nearer he never once turned to look at her.

Idly she speculated about the color of his eyes. Black, perhaps, to go with his dark hair. Maybe blue. Or . . .

Suddenly he turned his head and looked at her, and she was almost knocked off her feet by the answer to her question. *Green.* His eyes were so dark a green, they seemed to hold the approaching storm in them. She'd seen fine jade the color of his eyes. She'd also seen that same color in a forest at night, lit only by moonlight.

"Hello," he said, his voice deep and pleasant as he stood.

"Hello."

And his hair—a slash of silver streaked through his dark hair, starting at the right side of his forehead and running straight back. Extraordinary . . .

All at once, in a blur of motion, he was there next to her and she felt an iron arm around her, trapping her. She tried to scream, but a white cloth covered her nose and mouth and then she was breathing in a sickly-sweet odor.

All these years she'd been ready for something like this to happen, and then she'd gone and let herself be knocked off guard by a pair of green eyes.

The strength drained out of her and her vision faded, and disgust at herself mingled with a cold, cold fear.

She felt movement and heard a droning noise. A plane? How did she get on a plane?

"I don't want her to wake up yet," a deep voice said. "We've got hours yet."

She had heard his voice before. But where? She tried to open her eyes, but couldn't manage it. A chill gripped her, and fear knotted in her stomach and pressed in on her chest. She heard a whimper and realized it had come from her.

A hand smoothed over her forehead.

"Shhh," the voice said soothingly. The hand was gentle, but she felt a sharp prick on her arm and then she knew no more.

Sin stared down at her, remembering the fear in her eyes as she'd lost consciousness. He couldn't forget it. Fear was a basic emotion, one everyone was familiar with. He had seen it in many a man's eyes. Even a few women's.

But in her eyes, the fear had been very hard to look at. Maybe because when he'd first stood and turned toward her, her beautiful, clear gray eyes had held only an innocent curiosity. The fear had come seconds later when she had realized she'd been lured into a trap.

One moment there had been a wild beauty about her, with her butterscotch-and-caramel-colored hair whipping about her head, and her face, shining and relaxed. The next moment she'd been like a captured animal. It was a shame, but it couldn't be helped. He needed her and he was going to keep her until he didn't anymore.

As he pulled a blanket up over her his hand strayed to her cheek. Abruptly he straightened. "She's cold. Someone get me another blanket immediately."

Pain pounded relentlessly in her head. Her mouth was cotton dry. Her tongue felt swollen. Grit rasped against the back of her eyelids. Slowly she tried to open them and failed. God, what had happened to her? She tried again and after a great amount of effort finally succeeded.

Not that it did her any good. She hurt too much to move, and any moment now she was going to throw up. So she simply studied the ceiling and tried to arrange her thoughts.

The ceiling in her small apartment in Maine was a pale blue. She had chosen the color herself and painted it one Sunday afternoon last month. The ceiling above her now was much higher than the one in her apartment and a cream color.

She wasn't where she had expected to be.

So where was she? And why?

She remembered a pair of jade-green eyes; *they* held the answer.

The room was filled with natural light. The last thing she remembered was that night was coming on. How long had she been knocked out? Experimentally she moved slightly and was rewarded by a sharp jolt of pain piercing through her head.

"So you're finally awake."

The voice was smooth and deep and wasn't the one she had last heard. She shifted so that she could see who had spoken, but the pain proved too much, wrenching a moan from her.

"Hang on," the voice said. "I've got something that will help you."

He'd have to kill her to make her better, and she didn't know that he wouldn't. Fear threatened to suffocate her. She had to concentrate to make sure she kept breathing.

He leaned over her, his wide shoulders blocking out her view of the room. He was a big man with tawny coloring to his eyes and hair, and a peculiar silver streak running through his hair.

A silver streak? The man on the beach had had one too. But amber eyes? No, she thought. They had been green. This wasn't the man who had been on the beach, the man she very much wanted to see again, the man with her answers. And as soon as she got those answers, she was going to do her best to make his life as much of a hell as he had made hers.

"Where . . . where is—"

He slipped his arm beneath her shoulders, lifted her slightly, and held a glass of water to her lips. "Take a sip."

She supposed she should be cautious about his offer, but her parched throat cried out for relief and she felt too bad to deny herself. A sip proved the liquid to be cool water and she made a feeble attempt to drink more.

"Wait." He pulled the glass away. "Not too much at once." He then held a capsule to her lips. "Put this in your mouth and I'll give you another small drink."

Water was one thing, but unknown medication was another. She pressed her lips shut.

"Come on, Jillian," he said coaxingly. "I promise you this will make you feel better."

He knew her name. That ruled out the possibility that she had been kidnapped by mistake. What was going on? She didn't have a clue who he was and she had no reason to believe what he said. Her lips stayed closed.

"Think of it this way," he said, a touch of dry humor in his voice. "How much worse could you feel?"

He had a point, she thought. The pain in her head was fierce and her stomach roiled to the extent that she didn't think she'd ever be able to eat again. And since he and the green-eyed man hadn't killed her yet, chances were they might not anytime soon. She took the chance and swallowed the capsule.

"That's a good girl. You'll start to feel better soon."

If she'd had the strength she would have scratched his eyes out for that condescending "that's a good girl." And that was the least of his transgressions as far as she was concerned. But she didn't have the strength. She was in a world of trouble that she couldn't begin to get herself out of until she understood what that trouble was. Until she did, she needed to pick the fights she could win.

"Where am I?"

"Does it matter?"

She moistened her lips. "Vitally."

He drew up a chair beside the bed and sat down. "You're on a private island in the Pacific."

That piece of information made no sense to her. "Why?"

"You're going to be a guest of the Damaron family for a while."

"Guest?"

"Relax, Jillian. No one is going to harm you."

His smile held a charming laziness that was completely lost on her. "Harm me any more than I already have been, you mean?"

His smile faded. "I'm sorry we had to drug you, but we had no other choice."

"You're mistaken. *I'm* the one who was given no choice."

"As I said, I'm sorry."

"Where's the other man?"

He looked taken aback. "What other man?"

"The man on the beach. The man who chloroformed me."

"Ah, yes, that was my cousin Sin."

"Sin?" She wasn't surprised at the name.

After what he had done to her she could definitely believe he was a man well acquainted with sin.

"Sinclair Damaron. This is his house." He stood, apparently having given her all the information he was going to. "Get some rest, Jillian. You'll find everything you need in this room and the adjoining bath. When you wake up again pick up the phone and food will be brought to you." At the door, he turned around and looked at her. "But whatever you do, don't try to get away. You can't and you'll only end up hurting yourself."

"Wait. What's your name?"

"Lion. Lion Damaron." He left, shutting the door behind him.

She stared at the door, hardly able to believe her situation. A dark-haired man with jade-green eyes named Sin had chloroformed her on a beach in Maine and now she was on an island in the Pacific? And it wasn't a mistake. They knew her name.

Damaron. Obviously it was a name she should know, but it simply wasn't familiar to her.

She felt as if she had stepped into some sort of nightmare where reality had no place. She had to get out of the room she was being kept in, out of the house, and off the island.

She *had* to.

Being in a place or even a situation she

couldn't get out of was intolerable to her. Even now her heart was hammering with fear. She added deep, calming breaths to her list of things she had to concentrate on.

Closing her eyes, she willed the pain in her head to pass, her stomach to still, and her panic to ease. She would get out of this, she vowed. She had to. . . .

Sleep claimed her again, but sometime later she heard a voice, *the* voice. It pulled at her through the heavy darkness of her sleep.

"How is she?"

He was there beside her bed, the man called Sin.

She struggled to open her eyes, but the drugs in her system proved far stronger than her will and her eyes remained closed. She wanted to cry out in frustration. She wanted to look at him again and demand answers and some sort of satisfaction. She'd spent most of her life trying to remain free, but as quickly and as easily as saying hello to her, he had erased her sense of security and well-being. She couldn't allow him to get away with it.

"She'll be fine when she wakes up."

That was Lion speaking.

"Are you sure? She seems to be sleeping a lot."

"She's doing exactly what she's supposed to be doing, Sin. Sleep is the best thing for her. When she wakes up, her headache will be gone and she'll be ready to eat a full meal."

She tried again to open her eyes, but her lids felt as if they had been cemented shut. A soft moan escaped her lips.

"What's wrong? She's trying to wake up."

"But she won't. Not yet."

She felt a hand on her forehead, the same hand that had soothed her on the plane. Sin Damaron's touch was gentle, but it agitated her. God, how she hated feeling helpless.

He removed his hand. "And the doctor guaranteed the drugs were safe? You did double-check, didn't you?"

"Yes. Absolutely. Quit worrying. She's going to be fine."

"All right, then. Until this thing breaks open, make sure she's kept out of the way and has everything she needs."

It was the last thing she heard him say before sleep claimed her once again.

When she next opened her eyes, shadows were creeping across the room and her head no longer hurt. And it didn't take her long to realize that Lion had been right when he had told Sin that she would be hungry. She was starving. But the need to escape far outweighed her need to eat. She sat up and brushed her hair off her forehead.

Lion had told her she couldn't escape, but she didn't for a minute believe him. She'd taken several self-defense courses. Unfortunately those courses hadn't done her a lot of good on the beach, but then no course ever covered what to do when confronted by the most extraordinary green eyes she'd ever seen. Still she'd spent most of her life slipping free of traps. The question wasn't if she could escape, but when and how.

She simply had to find out where the weaknesses were and how much latitude, if any, she was going to be given. And as far as she was concerned, the man named Sin was the key. He'd said, *Make sure she has everything she needs*, as if he was delegating her to Lion. *Keep her out of the way*. Yeah, right. She would lose her mind if she sat and did nothing and simply accepted her fate. If Sin Damaron thought he could do something as hideously awful as kidnap her and then *ignore* her, he was dead wrong.

Carefully she slid off the bed to her feet. Dizziness swamped her. She waited until she felt steadier, then took a few experimental steps. "Damn him, whoever he is," she muttered, and headed for the door.

To her surprise, it wasn't locked. Moreover, there was no guard stationed in the hallway. Frowning over her discovery, she closed the door and started across the room to a set of French doors, but the sight of her suitcase sitting on a bench at the end of the bed made her detour. Inside it she found enough of her clothing and toiletries to last for an extended stay.

Sin Damaron had been in her apartment, gone through her things, packed them. How efficient. How terrifying.

Fear and fury almost paralyzed her. He had obviously put a great deal of thought into abducting her. But why? What had she done to him—or to *anyone*—to deserve this? She'd been living her life as quietly as she knew how, bothering no one, doing nothing to attract anyone's attention. And then this man . . .

Tears stung at the back of her throat. Whatever game Sin Damaron was playing, she couldn't let him win. She *couldn't*.

She grabbed a few things out of the bag and headed for the bathroom. She didn't need to know the exact length of time she'd been wearing the jeans and sweater she had on to guess that it had been too long. She showered in the spacious cream-and-gold marble shower, then changed into a clean pair of jeans and a T-shirt. She felt a tiny bit more in control of her situation, no matter how much she realized that feeling might be an illusion.

A second check of the hall outside her door showed it still to be empty. They must be very sure she couldn't escape, she thought grimly. Next she tried the French doors.

They were locked, but from the inside. With a flick of her finger, she unlocked them and pushed the doors outward.

A balmy breeze rushed over her, caressing her skin and ruffling her still-wet hair as she walked out onto a small private terrace that overlooked a stretch of green lawn and an endless expanse of azure sea. An island in the Pacific, Lion had said.

It might as well have been the moon, for all the sense it made.

Then she saw him, standing several levels and terraces below her, staring out at the sea, just as he had been doing the first time she had seen him, as if he saw a storm approaching. Yet the coming night was clear and falling gently in shades of lavender and gray.

Without further thought she took the steps that led downward from one terrace to another until she reached the level he was at.

"Why have you done this to me?"

Jolted, Sin Damaron spun around. "You're awake," he said.

She'd seen his eyes only once, but she hadn't forgotten their power and deep, dark color. And now she saw her memory had been correct. "Yes, I'm awake—finally—no thanks to you and the drugs you used on me." Her voice shook with rage and more desperation than she cared to reveal, but there was nothing she could do about it. "How *dare* you drug me and bring me here without my permission? Who are you and why have you done this to me? *Why?*"

Instead of answering her, he looked past her shoulder and held up a hand.

She glanced around and saw striding purposefully toward them a young man with copper-colored skin and Rastafarian braids. "Your bodyguard?"

"A good friend of the family. His name is David."

Her hands clenched into fists at her side to keep from hitting him. "I don't care what his name is. And what's more, it might be better for you if he *was* your bodyguard."

A very faint smile touched his lips. "If that was a threat, I'll ignore it."

Pain scored her throat as she swallowed the scream rising inside her. But screaming would gain her nothing, except perhaps more mind-numbing, sleep-inducing drugs. "Just tell me why you've done this to me and then I want to go back home. *Immediately.*"

Sinclair nodded, studying her closely. The fear was still there in the clear gray eyes, along with the enormous effort she was making to keep it at bay. Silently he saluted her and, at the same time, found himself annoyed. She should never have been able to catch him unaware as she had. Maybe he should rethink his decision not to confine her to her room.

He had a lot on his mind and he didn't need to be sidetracked by her.

He tilted his head to one side and rubbed a finger against his temple, a habit whose genesis was in weariness rather than pain. During the last week he had been working practically around the clock, making and implementing the plan.

"I can understand why you want to know, and you will be told. First, though, you should probably eat something." He gestured toward the house. "If you'll just go in, I'll see to it—"

"*No.* I won't just *anything* until you tell me what I want to know."

"After you eat." He glanced again at David. "David, tell Jacqueline to prepare dinner for Jillian and serve it in the lounge. She'll be there in a minute."

"I'll only go into the house if you go too. I want answers."

"David will—"

"No, *you* will. *You're* the one who kidnapped me. *You're* the one who needs to tell me."

He took in her defiant stance with thoughtfulness. Even mild intelligence would dictate prudence. Wasn't she aware that with one lift of a finger, he could have her drugged again? Not that he would, but she couldn't know that. She had to be operating on pure instinct. Sensing that he wanted to be rid of the responsibility of her, she was determined to stick with him.

"I didn't kidnap you single-handedly, Jillian. It was a group effort."

"A group effort? A *group*?" She stopped herself, took a deep breath, then started again. "I didn't see a group of *anything* on that beach, holding a rag soaked with chloroform. I saw *you.*"

Emotion flushed her skin rose and set fascinating lights sparkling in her eyes. Angry energy vibrated off her in waves, giving her an incredible aura of vibrancy. He had the odd notion that if he reached out and touched her he wouldn't be able to withstand the electrical jolt he would receive. Even odder, he still wanted to touch her. But he wouldn't.

She was nothing more than a means to an end to him, and nothing or no one would be allowed to interfere with that end. Still, if he answered her questions now, she'd be easier for the others to handle from this point on.

Reluctantly he nodded at David. "Tell Jacqueline I'll be eating too."

TWO

Jillian didn't know whether or not it had been wise for her to stick her neck out and insist that Sin answer her questions, but for whatever reason, he was willing to let her have her way on this. She wasn't certain what it meant, or even if it meant anything, but she decided to see how much further she could push things. If nothing else, it was a quick way to locate boundaries. She had to start somewhere figuring things out, and to her, Sinclair Damaron was the obvious place to start.

He led her to a large room done in rattan, mahogany, and chintz and seated her at an oval table by a window that stretched the length of the room. The view beyond showed dark jewel colors of deep purple, royal blue, and black jade. If she'd been on a holiday she would have been mesmerized by the beauty, but that was far from the case. She was being held there against her will, and now that she had had a chance to take more than a cursory look at the view, she could detect what she had missed before—men strategically placed along the beach. Their casual dress gave no indication of the weapons they might be carrying, but she had no doubt that they were well armed. Occasionally she would see one of them lift a walkie-talkie to speak into it.

"For me?" she asked, indicating the men.

"In a roundabout way." He spread a linen napkin across his knee.

"Do you honestly think it takes an island with armed guards to keep one woman from escaping?" Her voice sounded uneven from the effort of keeping her distress in check.

"I'm not afraid that you'll escape."

"You should be, because first chance I get, I will."

"Jillian, Jillian—haven't you ever learned that it's not good to tip your hand to an enemy?"

She wondered if he was aware of the unexpectedly soft way he said her name. If he was, it was probably meant to put her off her guard and she refused to buy into it. "I learned, but you'll forgive me if I'm not exactly thinking straight." She ignored the wine he had poured for her. "None of this makes any sense."

"No?"

"*No*. What about me is so valuable to you that you would go to this effort to kidnap me and bring me thousands of miles to this place?"

"You really have no idea?"

"I don't have a clue."

"I find that hard to believe."

"And I find that I don't care *what* you believe. It's the truth. I don't even have a guess why I'm here. It can't be money. I don't have any, especially compared to what you must have." She gestured at her surroundings.

"You're right. It's not money."

She stared at him, her brow knitted in concentration. The gaze he returned was impenetrable, unfathomable. She would defy *anyone* to read this man's mind. "I didn't think it was the money. I also don't think that somehow you developed some sort of undying, from-a-distance passion for me and decided to kidnap me for your very own."

Sin had to smile at that. He didn't have any idea what sort of romantic liaisons she had been involved in, but she obviously had never looked at herself through a man's eyes. He, himself, had had the chance to observe her for only about twenty-four hours before he snatched her, but it had actually taken just one look to be intrigued. He'd seen the quick natural way she laughed with her customers at the restaurant where she worked and how equally quick she was to rush to help someone. He'd seen the sexy picture she made as she strode around the little coastal town in her jeans, sweater, and very little makeup, full of energy and vitality, uncaring that her hair was blowing wildly.

Right now that hair, an odd, wonderful color of butterscotch and caramel, looked silky soft, tossed by the breeze into fetching disorder. It tempted him, making him want to run his fingers through it to see if he could bring order to it.

The pale pink color of her T-shirt picked up the rose undertone of her skin, and the cotton knit material hugged the rounded curves of her full breasts and showed the faint outline of her nipples. She was a compelling, alluring woman.

"Is it really that hard to believe a man would develop an undying passion for you, Jillian?"

"Yes."

She sounded so definite, and he wondered why. Was she that naive? Didn't she know she could make a man's loins swell with just a toss of her head or a gray-eyed look full of laughter, or blazing anger. "Perhaps you should look in the mirror again."

She slowly shook her head. "You didn't kidnap me for that reason."

No, he hadn't, he silently agreed. But that didn't mean he didn't find her tempting. He cursed at himself. What was he doing, drawing this matter out? She'd gotten him off-track, something he hadn't thought possible under the circumstances. "You're right, I didn't."

She leaned forward. "Then what? What is it you want?"

"I want Steffan Wythe."

The name knocked the breath out of her and she felt the blood drain from her face. Somewhere deep inside her, in a place she had been refusing to let herself access, she'd known her stepfather had something to do with what had happened to her. In fact, when she'd awakened earlier that day, she had been surprised not to find herself in her yellow bedroom in Steffan's house in the Middle East.

"No." It was the first thing she found she wanted to say, the *only* thing she wanted to say.

"Yes," he said mildly. "I want Wythe and I plan to get him."

A burning tightness gripped her chest, a roaring filled her ears. Slowly she eased back against the chair. "And you think that when he hears that you've kidnapped me he'll come after me?"

"That's what I think."

"Well, you're wrong." She prayed to God he was wrong. He *had* to be wrong.

He shook his head. "I don't think so. In fact, I think you're pretty much the only thing in the world that would make him come out of exile."

He tore his gaze from her to smile at a tall, older woman who had entered the room, followed by a younger man who wheeled out their dinner on a cart. "Jacqueline, thank you for preparing us something to eat on such short notice."

"It was no trouble at all," she said.

"Jacqueline, this is Jillian Wythe. She's going to be with us for a while."

Jacqueline stood back, while the younger man deftly served them. "How do you do, Miss Wythe."

Manners taught to her long ago by her mother made Jillian manage a nod in the older woman's direction.

"And," Sin said, continuing, "her young helper is her nephew, Clay."

Jillian dropped an unseeing gaze to the plate in front of her, feeling hysteria threatening. She found it ludicrous that Sin was making introductions as if they were in a social situation. Jacqueline and Clay had to know that she was being held there against her will. She picked up the knife from beside her plate. What kind of people were they, who, without a qualm or question, would serve dinner to someone who was being kept a prisoner by their employer?

"Do you now have a better idea how long Miss Wythe will be a guest?" Jacqueline asked Sin, obviously having decided she would get no response from Jillian.

"No, but I still don't think it will be too long."

Jillian had more than enough to be angry about without summoning any indignation that they were talking about her over her head. Absently she looked at the knife, as her thumb rubbed back and forth across its dull edge. Finding out the reason she had been kidnapped had been a huge shock and had left only one real thought in her head: There was no way she could allow Steffan to come get her. She had to escape first.

"Thank you, Jacqueline, Clay," Sin murmured as they left the room. "Aren't you going to eat, Jillian?"

Slowly she refocused on Sin and their surroundings and she realized they were once again alone. Carefully she put down the knife. Even if it were sharp, it probably wouldn't have done her any good. "He won't come," she said softly. "Steffan hasn't been out of the Middle East in years." It was the one thing on her side she had to hold on to, the one reason she had been so successful in keeping his

name in the back of her mind when she'd
been trying to figure out why she had been
kidnapped.

"He doesn't have to leave to see you because you fly back there at regular intervals.
But when he learns that you're being held
here against your will, I'm betting he'll come.
Our information tells us he loves you very
much."

"And I'm telling you he *won't* come. He
considers leaving to be too dangerous for
him."

"I'm aware of that. But when the life of
his beloved stepdaughter is involved, he'll ignore the danger."

She shook her head, wanting above everything to negate what he was saying. "My—my
mother. She's very ill."

"I know and I'm sorry."

She couldn't detect an ounce of sincerity
in his voice or a glint of sympathy in his eyes.
She looked away. The room they were in was
enormous and the view beyond the window
endless, but it was evening now, and even
though the grounds were lit, all she could see
was darkness. She felt as if the walls and the
dark night were closing in on her. Soon, she
thought, she wouldn't be able to keep the hysteria from swamping her.

"Daddy! Daddy!"

Jillian started as a little girl rushed into the

room in a whirl of blond curls, chubby little arms and legs, and bare feet, and headed straight for Sin's outstretched arms.

Effortlessly he scooped her onto his lap and kissed her silky head. "And exactly what are you doing up, my darling Lily?"

Hearing his deep, hard voice soften with indulgence came as a shock to Jillian. In fact, the child was a shock.

Dressed in a ruffled, flower-sprigged nightgown, the angelic vision giggled, then stuck her lower lip out in an irresistible pout. "You didn't come tuck me in."

"That's right, because I made a deal with you. I said if you'd let Reena tuck you in tonight that tomorrow we'd do something special together. Remember?"

"No." She drew the one word out in a sweet singsong tone and cuddled back against him as if he were a pillow. A narrow silver streak ran through her baby-fine hair, obviously inherited from her father, along with the big green eyes that she fixed on Jillian. "Hi," she said shyly.

For the life of her, Jillian could summon no response. The appearance of the child in the middle of what was essentially an armed camp couldn't have been more unexpected or out of place to her. Plus she was astounded by the ease with which the child cuddled in the arms of the man who had abducted her so cold-bloodedly.

"Jillian," Sin said, his voice carrying a note of warning, "this is my daughter, Lily. Lily, this is Miss Wythe. She's going to be our guest for a while."

He didn't want her to upset his daughter, but he needn't have worried. She couldn't think of a thing to say.

"Can she play with me?" Lily asked.

"No. Miss Wythe is going to be too busy, but I will. I will, that is, if you'll go back to your room now." Cradling the little girl, he reached around to the table behind him, picked up the phone, and punched a number. "Reena," he said, "Lily is in the lounge with me. Would you please come take her back to bed? Thank you." He hung up and looked down at his daughter. "You're a little minx, aren't you?"

"Yes," she said, giggling, her shoulders hunched, her hand raised coyly over her mouth, a natural coquette where her father was concerned.

Jillian could only conclude that he cared deeply for his own child. But really the fact told her almost nothing. Even the wildest and most predatory of animals protected their young, and he was still very much her enemy. An *attractive* enemy, she reflected grudgingly, observing the softness in his face as he talked to his daughter, but an enemy nevertheless.

"Reena is coming to get you," he said to Lily. "If you'll go get in bed, I promise I'll come and kiss you good night in just a little while."

"How long is that?" she asked, beaming a cherubic smile up at him.

"Not long." He kissed her cheek.

A heavyset woman with a serene expression entered the room, wearing a long, floral dress cut in the native South Seas style. "Ah, so there you are, my little one." She shook a gentle finger at her charge. "I turn my back and, *poof*, you disappear, just like a fairy sprite." Lily giggled and held out her arms. "I'm sorry, Mr. Damaron," Reena said, once she had Lily in her arms.

"No problem this time, but please, it's very important to keep a close eye on her during these next few days."

"I understand, Mr. Damaron. I'm going to move my bed into her room tonight. I will be between her and the door."

"Get someone to help you. Lily," he said, "remember, go to bed and I'll be in soon."

Oblivious to the worry she had caused, the little girl rubbed at her eyes. "But what if I'm asleep?"

"I'll wake you up."

With a sweet smile, she laid her head on her nanny's shoulder. "Okay."

When they left the room, Sin picked up his fork and began eating as if they hadn't been interrupted.

Jillian finally found her voice. "You have your daughter in a place where, if things go as you expect, a war will break out shortly?"

"Yes."

"But aren't you worried for her safety?"

He looked up at her. "More than I can begin to tell you. But I'd rather have her here, where I can personally keep her safe to the best of my ability, than have her somewhere else, out of my reach, in case Steffan goes after her. And he would if he thought he could."

"Go after Lily. But why?"

"Oh, come on, Jillian. Surely you know that when Steffan realizes I've taken you, his first response will be to want an eye for an eye. He'll look around to see what he can hit that will hurt me or that will give him bargaining power. Lily is the only thing I couldn't survive losing and that's why she's here with me." And with that remarkable statement he went back to eating.

She stared down at her own plate again without seeing what was there. After a moment she said, "Why?"

"Why what?"

"Why have you set this trap for Steffan?"

He hesitated, then leaned back in his chair, bringing his wineglass with him. "Are you sure you want to know? It's not a pretty story and it may blow your image of your beloved Steffan."

"May?"

"Yes, if you believe me. Or if you haven't already heard the story from him and accepted it."

She exhaled a deep breath. She was one nerve short of falling completely apart, but she had no place to retreat. She had to know everything before she could decide the best course of action to take. "Tell me."

He nodded. "Okay. How old were you fifteen, almost sixteen years ago?"

"About eleven, I guess," she said, surprised at the question.

"And at the time your mother had been married to Wythe—what?—about five years?"

"Yes."

He nodded. "I was nineteen, almost twenty when it happened."

If there was some line of thought that she was supposed to be following, she was failing miserably. "When *what* happened?"

"When your stepfather paid a well-known terrorist to plant a bomb on the family plane that was taking my parents, along with all my aunts and uncles, to a business meeting in Switzerland."

She stared at him, dumbfounded. "A what?"

Sin would have been surprised if she had known, but her blank look confirmed that she didn't. He was glad, and he didn't bother to stop and question why. "In one fell swoop, your stepfather killed an entire generation of my family. That bomb blew their plane out of the sky, and all because of a longtime rivalry and an important business deal he would lose if their plane had been allowed to land in Switzerland."

Jillian could only sit there, looking stunned and numb.

Taking a sip of his wine, he never once let his gaze stray from her. It was clear he'd shocked her. "I see you're having a hard time believing it, but I can assure you it's the truth. Vergara was the name of the terrorist who did the job for Wythe—you may have heard of him—and he has confessed to everything."

"Now? After all these years, he's confessed? Why now?"

"Because my cousin Jonah, after years spent tracking him down, finally caught him. And because our family has promised Vergara that his family's future will be secured if he will tell everything."

"Is that legal?"

Sin threw back his head and laughed harshly. "I've just told you that your stepfather killed my family and you ask if it's legal to ensure that two little boys have enough money to eat and be educated? Is your loyalty to Wythe really that blind?"

She laced her shaking fingers together and lowered them to her lap. "You can't expect me to hear those things and not be stunned."

"Stunned by what your stepfather did? You must have had at least a hint over the years that he could be capable of such extreme evil. Wythe raised you, didn't he? You lived in his house."

Sin silently cursed. It had been a deliberately cruel thing for him to say and totally unnecessary. Wythe was a father figure to her, not the monster he was to the Damaron family. Hurting her more than he already had would accomplish nothing. "I'm sorry. I shouldn't have said that."

He waited a moment, but when she didn't say anything, he set his wineglass on the table and considered her. Strangely, he never expected to be touched by her. But something about her made him remember he had a conscience, made him remember he was a man. All in all she was proving damned inconvenient.

He rubbed the back of his neck where his muscles had tightened to the point of pain.

For years, he and his cousins had been working toward this point. It was vitally important
to all of them that the man responsible for the
death of their parents be brought to justice,
whether the court's justice or their own.
They'd long suspected it had been Wythe
who had given the orders for the bomb. Once
Vergara had provided the confirmation, the
gloves had come off and anyone connected to
Wythe had become fair game.

It had been hard, because after the plane
explosion, Wythe had wisely retreated to a
Middle Eastern country with no extradition
treaty with the United States, a country that
would appreciate the money he was willing to
pour into their till and allow him to live like a
king. So he and his family had had to come up
with a way to lure him out.

And Jillian had gotten caught in the cross
fire.

Now that he'd seen her, watched her,
looked into her gray eyes, he discovered he
couldn't be quite as dispassionate about her as
he would like. But he hoped it would all be
over very quickly, and in the meantime he had
an island full of people who could take care of
her. As soon as Wythe showed up, they'd nab
him and she could go back to her life, as
strange a life as he found it to be for a stepdaughter of Wythe's, waiting tables for a liv-

ing and living in a small three-room apartment.

"Eat," he said brusquely. "You don't want to become sick."

No, she didn't, Jillian thought, but she also didn't think she *could* eat. For the first time she managed to focus on the food before her, and she discovered some sort of fish on her plate, with a sauce that contained almonds. Her stomach turned over at the sight. "I can't eat this."

"Why not?"

She said the first thing that came into her head. "I'm . . . I'm allergic to seafood of any kind."

He reached for the phone and punched out a number. "Jacqueline, Miss Wythe is allergic to seafood. Please bring her something else." He glanced at her. "Is there anything in particular you would like?"

"Yes, I'd like to be taken home."

His mouth tightened. "Make her one of your wonderful omelettes, Jacqueline. Thank you." He hung up the phone and tossed his napkin onto the table. "You should have said something sooner, but it doesn't matter. She'll have your omelette out here as soon as possible. In the meantime I have things to do and I—"

"I'm allergic to eggs."

Already half out of his seat, he dropped back down. "You're allergic to eggs?"

"That's right."

"I see." A muscle moved along his jawline. "Then what can you eat?"

"I can eat the food back in Maine."

"We have the same food here. All you have to do is tell me what you *can* eat."

She had annoyed him. Good. He had been about to dismiss her, but she didn't plan to let him, not if she could help it. He'd turned her life upside down. He'd made her into a weapon that would bring his enemy down. And in return, he expected her to behave, not to give him trouble, not to make any waves. The least she could do was see that he was sorely disappointed in that regard.

"Jillian?"

"I've already told you—I can eat the food back in Maine."

He reached for the phone. "Forget the omelette, Jacqueline. I'll get back to you in a minute." He hung up and turned to her. "Exactly what is it you think you are going to gain by not eating?"

She had every intention of eating, just as she had every intention of making his life miserable until he let her go or she found some way to escape. But his next carefully measured words made her doubt that she would even come close to success on either score.

"I don't have a lot of time to spend humoring you, Jillian, nor do I have the inclination, so just listen and understand. Under no circumstances will you be taken back to Maine until I have Wythe where I want him. And *until* that time you will be kept here. I've given instructions that you are to have everything you need to make you comfortable. To that end, Jacqueline will prepare anything you desire, but if you don't want to eat, then I'm not going to waste a lot of energy trying to make you. On the other hand, I also don't plan to watch you starve. If you refuse to eat, I'll simply have you fed intravenously."

How could such amazing eyes go so cold and so hard? she wondered. "You wouldn't."

"I would." He stood up and looked down at her. "In short, it's up to you how pleasant your stay here will be. Or how unpleasant."

Shaking with anger, she surged to her feet. "Pleasant? *Pleasant?* Damn you, I'm a *prisoner* here."

"Yes, you are, but you won't be kept in chains. You can have the run of the house and its immediate grounds and there's plenty here to keep you amused. Perhaps you should consider this a vacation."

"A vacation?" She almost sputtered.

He smiled. "Good night, Jillian. You found your way out of your bedroom. I trust you can find your way back."

She sank back into the chair a second before her knees buckled. God, what was she going to do? Tears sprang into her eyes and she angrily brushed them away. She had to think. . . .

"Miss Wythe?"

Her head jerked up and she saw Jacqueline standing before her. "What?"

"You must eat something," the woman said gently.

"I—I can't."

"I understand—your stomach is upset just now. Perhaps a nice soothing consommé. I will bring it, and if you find you cannot tolerate that, we will try something else until we find something you can tolerate."

The woman's unexpected kindness made her want to cry, but then she realized that Jacqueline was simply trying to follow her employer's orders. Still, there was no point in being rude to her when it was Sin Damaron she wanted to suffer. She nodded. "Thank you, Jacqueline."

THREE

Jillian sat in the middle of the bed, every light in the room on. The bedside clock informed her it was a little after one in the morning.

Sleep had always been a problem for her. She fought it like a tiger. When she did succumb, she slept lightly and then for only a few hours at a time.

Odd that she felt tired, she reflected; she'd slept most of the last day due to the drugs. Then again perhaps it wasn't so surprising. She had been through a great deal of trauma since her afternoon beach walk in Maine.

Steffan had killed an entire generation of Sin's family.

The idea was giving her nightmares even though she was wide-awake. Her mind couldn't quite grasp it. She knew many things about Steffan, but she certainly hadn't known that. It was too horrible to contemplate, too *evil*, just as Sin had said. If Steffan had indeed been responsible . . .

If . . .

Her mind couldn't take that additional step to finish the thought.

She looked around her. The room was comfortable, done in creams and gold. The bed appeared to have a down mattress pad and was covered with finely woven sheets and mounds of pillows. It would probably be heaven to sleep in. To help her relax even further, she'd changed into her own oversized sleep shirt that she'd found in the suitcase.

Still, she couldn't bring herself to the point of relinquishing consciousness. In fact, the thought frightened her. At present she only had control of herself, and if she went to sleep she would have to relinquish even that.

She slid off the bed and hurried over to the French doors to double-check that she had locked them from the inside. She had. Next she doubled-checked the door that led to the hall. It was locked too.

Chewing on her bottom lip, she wrapped her arms around her waist and stared at the doorknob. The locks wouldn't keep her safe. They would keep no one out who really wanted in.

Her skin felt flushed and tight. Her heart was pounding. It was no use. She was too upset to sleep. And she couldn't bear to be closed up in this room.

She opened the door and stepped out into the hall, lit by a series of wall sconces. There was no guard, but knowing what she knew now, she was positive that even in the middle of the night, there were men protecting the house and grounds. But they weren't there in the hall and therefore wouldn't bother her.

She had no particular destination in mind as she started off, but since she hadn't yet been able to get a sense of the layout of the house, she might as well put this time to use. She studied each door as she passed, wondering who, if anyone, slept behind it. As soon as possible she also needed to figure out how many people were on the island. In fact, there were a great many things she needed to learn if she was going to be able to escape. If . . .

She stopped as she noticed the set of carved mahogany doors at the end of the hall. The master suite, perhaps? She eyed the double doors speculatively, wondering if Sin was behind them and, if so, if was he sleeping.

She frowned in irritation. Of course he was sleeping. *He* was the one who had the control. She had none. There was nothing fair or right about the position she was in. It was even more unfair that he should be getting rest while she roamed the halls, sleepless. Still, she hesitated. She would be taking a huge chance to try to undermine his control. On the other hand, how much more trouble could she get into?

She tested the doorknob. Unlocked, it turned. Carefully she slipped inside.

The room was dark, and she waited a few moments while her eyes adjusted. She could sense Sin's presence. It was something about the air that convinced her—a hint of warm musky skin, a touch of masculine sexuality, a trace of dark spice. And there was the faint sound of deep, even breathing.

Lord, she had to be out of her mind to have broken into his bedroom while he slept. In the clear light of day she would probably have been able to talk herself out of the idea. But it was the middle of the night and she was angry, not to mention upset and very afraid. She was running on nerves and raw emotions. And it was *his* fault. Dammit, he couldn't simply toy with a person's life and get off scot-free. No matter what his reasons were. No matter who he was.

He had put her in an impossible, intolerable position, and she was having to suffer the consequences. It seemed only right that he suffer along with her.

She tiptoed across the room to the big bed and eased herself onto it until she sat near his feet, her legs tucked beneath her. It had been easy, she thought, congratulating herself. Too easy.

She heard the deadly sound of a revolver being cocked, followed by his deep, harsh voice. "Don't move."

Ice slipped down her spine. "I don't plan to."

He moved quickly, turning on the bedside lamp and sitting up. All the while his gun was pointed straight at her heart.

A series of curses turned the air blue when he saw her. "What in the hell do you think you're doing, coming in here like this?"

"I couldn't sleep," she said, unable to tear her gaze away from the barrel of the gun.

He blinked. "You couldn't *what*?"

"I couldn't sleep. I—I couldn't get comfortable. Could you please point that gun somewhere else."

With a tilt of his wrist, he uncocked it and laid it on the bedside table. "This was a damned stupid thing for you to do, Jillian. I could have shot you."

That particular circumstance had occurred to her, but she had trusted that he wouldn't. Because tonight, as she sat alone in her bedroom, she had become aware of something. For whatever reason, *she wasn't afraid of Sin, only of the situation he had put her into.*

For many reasons and on many levels, she

was terrified of the situation. But not of Sin. It didn't make sense, but there it was.

"I didn't think it was fair that you should be able to sleep if I couldn't."

"Fair?" He rubbed his face, then shifted his position, drawing the covers up to his waist. "And you crept into my room—why? Do you want something to help you sleep?"

"More drugs? Lord, *no.*"

"Then what do you want?"

"Want? I told you—"

"I know. You don't think it's fair."

"It's not."

He exhaled a heavy breath. "Okay, then, *why* can't you sleep?"

"You mean besides the fact that you're holding me here against my will?"

"Besides that."

She searched her mind for something that would seem likely. "Ummm, it's the pillow. There aren't any comfortable pillows on my bed. I'm used to a certain type of pillow and I can't sleep without it."

He'd been dreaming about her, Sin realized, though he couldn't remember the substance of the dream. She'd simply been there, much as she was now, filling up all the space, so that all he saw was her, her hair soft and tousled, her eyes solemn and fearful, her skin gleaming and infinitely touchable.

What he hadn't seen in his dream was

what she would look like in a sleep shirt, sitting on his bed, her legs tucked beneath her, her hands folded primly in her lap. Pale blue and oversized, the sleep shirt hung loose over her body and fell to just below her hips, covering everything that should be covered. But it clung to the rounded softness of her breasts, making it clear she wasn't wearing a bra, and left bare a long expanse of leg that made his throat go dry at the sight.

Sitting on his bed in the middle of the night was *not* the best place for her to be, at least it wasn't best for *him*. Quite simply her presence was playing havoc with his nervous system. With a sigh he rubbed his face again. "What kind of pillow do you want, Jillian?"

She shrugged. "One that's not too firm, not too soft. Oh, and it can't be too plump either, and I hate thin pillows."

"Seems like we have a problem." He nodded resignedly. "Okay. This is a big house with a great number of bedrooms. I'm sure somewhere there's a pillow you can sleep with." He threw back the covers and slid to his feet.

"Wait," she said, startled. "What are you doing?"

He glanced at her over his shoulder. "I'm getting up so that we can go find you a pillow."

Jillian swallowed. In the lamplight she

could plainly see his lean, muscular body, clad only in boxers. *Silk* boxers. *Short* silk boxers.

She didn't have to reach out and touch his legs to know that they were rock hard. She didn't need to run her fingers through the dark hair that covered his broad chest to know that it would be soft. She didn't need to stare at the front of his boxers to know what she would see there. And yet she wanted to do all those things. How incredibly stupid of her. On the beach, her very first impression of him had been power in repose. She hadn't known the half of it then. "I didn't mean . . ." Her words trailed off. "Maybe I should ask Jacqueline."

"Never mind," he said, drawing on a pair of pants and zipping them. "I'm up now. Let's go."

She was suddenly aware that she was feeling a different kind of tension, the tension of an intimacy brought about by being with a half-dressed man in a quiet house in the middle of the night. And all she had on was her nightshirt. She slid off the bed to her feet and tugged down the shirt around her thighs. "Uh, I'd better run back to my bedroom and get dressed."

"Don't worry about it," he said. "You can use one of my shirts as a cover-up."

"No, that's okay—"

"Here, use this one." He walked to her

and placed the shirt he'd had on earlier around her shoulders. His hands lingered longer than they should have as he unnecessarily adjusted the shirt. "So you honestly think the right pillow will help you sleep?"

That everything had to be absolutely right before she could sleep was true, but now she was sorry she had brought it up. And doubly sorry she had come into his room. He was standing too close, and the scents she had picked up when she first entered the room were stronger with him beside her, making warmth curl through her. "I hope so."

"Then let's go."

Silently she followed him, and as they made their way along the hallway, he motioned to three doors. "This suite is for Reena and Lily."

Close to him, which made sense. "What about this door?"

"Lion is using that bedroom, but no one is in here." He opened another door and, after switching on the light, waited while she passed through. "Try out those pillows."

Feeling incredibly awkward, she walked to the bed. She could feel his gaze on her—it heated her skin. And made it hard to remember her reasoning in seeking him out. Whatever it had been, it had been a mistake, because *she* was the one being bothered and agitated.

After feeling the fourth pillow, she said, "No, these won't do at all."

"Okay." Sin knew he had to get her back into her bedroom away from him before he did something he'd regret. Whatever discomfort she was feeling at going on a tour of bedrooms with him in the middle of the night couldn't begin to compare with *his* discomfort. Tomorrow, he vowed, he would have Jacqueline sit down with her and discuss every possible need she might have. Then he wouldn't have to worry about her anymore and he could concentrate on Wythe. Although he was beginning to wonder if that was possible. He'd already learned she wasn't a woman easily managed or ignored. To make it worse, she was a woman much too easily desired.

"There's one more bedroom in this wing we can try."

She nodded and followed him out. "So no one else is staying in this wing?"

"No."

"What about that man David?"

"If he's still here, he's in another area."

"*If* he's still here?"

"If he's on schedule, he flew out of here this evening."

He opened the last doorway off the hall and watched as she headed to the bed to squeeze and tweak the new pillows. He'd never thought one of his shirts could look so good, so beguiling, so unintentionally sexy. "Find anything you like?"

"No." Jillian had told the truth when she'd said that her pillow needed to be just right in order for her to sleep, so she went about testing each pillow very seriously. Unfortunately not one was even close. She turned to him. "Do you have any more?"

His lips twisted wryly. "You know, I thought I'd packed everything you'd need, but I never once considered your pillow."

She noted the way amusement lightened his eyes and softened his face. Regarding him as a very attractive man rather than her kidnapper was dangerous. But being attracted to him would never happen, because she wouldn't *let* it happen. He was her enemy. "Perhaps next time you kidnap someone you'll be better prepared."

"There won't be a next time," he said, all traces of humor vanishing. He held the door open for her. "Come on. I think there are several bedrooms on the other side of the house not being used."

"Where is your security force staying?"

"My cousins all have their own homes on the island. The guards are divided among the houses."

Out in the hall, she stopped and looked

back at him. "How large is this island anyway? And how many cousins do you have?"

The humor returned to his eyes. "The island is a nice size for an island—it belongs to the entire family—and I have quite a few cousins. Anything else you want to know?"

He had seen through her attempt to gather information, but it was all right, because she *had* learned some things that would probably prove useful to her. "Are all your cousins on the island now?"

"No, but those who aren't are being protected."

Because of Steffan. The Damarons were worried that instead of, or maybe in addition to, trying to get her off the island, Steffan would strike out at the Damarons. A chill shuddered through her. If Steffan had indeed been responsible for the bomb aboard the Damaron plane, then they were probably right. Suddenly she was swamped by weariness. "I think I'll go back to my room."

"But you haven't found a pillow yet."

"I'll just have to make do."

He studied her for a moment. "Are you all right?"

She actually managed a weak laugh. "No, I'm not. Not even close."

He took her elbow and guided her back down the hall toward the set of double doors. "You didn't try my pillows."

"No. It's all right—"

"It won't take that long."

There were six pillows on his bed. Under his watchful gaze, she checked all of them, and amazingly enough the last one she picked up was perfect. She held it up. "This one."

"Fine. Take it. Use it."

"Thank you." She started out the door when she remembered his shirt. She slipped out of it and handed it to him. "Thank you." She was thanking him when by rights she should be screaming at him, perhaps even trying to get his gun to force him to take her back to Maine. But right now she felt as if all the fight had been taken out of her.

"Sure. Do you think you'll be able to sleep now?"

She nodded tiredly. She knew she was going to need every last ounce of strength she could muster if she was going to get through this ordeal in one piece.

She looked lost, Sin thought, and very vulnerable. It was his fault. How could he have asked her if she was all right? Of course she wasn't, he thought, disgusted with himself. And still, he found he was reluctant to let her go. "I understand Jacqueline found something you could eat."

She hugged the pillow against herself. "That's right."

"Good. I'm glad. When you wake up in

the morning, lift the phone receiver and you'll get Jacqueline."

"No—" She stopped, then said simply "Good night," and left, closing the door behind her.

He stared at the door for a moment, then walked over to the bed and the shirt she had tossed there. It still held the warmth from her body, and as he inhaled, their mingled scents filled his senses. There was musk, spice . . . and a subtle hint of a floral fragrance and vanilla.

His eyelids lowered as his fist closed on the material, and he felt his body harden. She was the stepdaughter of his enemy, she was his captive. He wanted her, but he couldn't take her. He *wouldn't.*

FOUR

Sin's gaze swept back and forth across the horizon, then returned to Lily and Reena, who were walking slowly along the water's edge, looking for additions to Lily's seashell collection. Their morning walks were routine. He couldn't see any reason to curtail Lily's normal activities, at least for today. Tomorrow would probably be another matter.

Beyond them, a sleek white, specially equipped speedboat with two armed men slowly glided parallel to the beach. Two other men stood within yards of Lily. Most of the island defenses were concealed, but where Lily was concerned, Sin took no chances.

The waiting—Lord, how he hated it. He had done everything there was to be done. The trap had been set, and now they had to wait for their prey to show up. He wasn't kidding himself. Nothing about this was going to be easy.

Footsteps sounded on the terrace behind him and he swung around to see Lion striding toward him. "Any sign yet that Wythe's on the move?"

"None so far." Lion dropped down into a chair at a table set for breakfast. "But I'm betting it won't be long now." He poured himself a glass of orange juice and drank it down. "Our sources tell us that he began to monitor the situation as soon as Vergara was taken into custody. He had to know he was about to be exposed."

"You're sure he got the message about Jillian?"

"Oh, yeah, he knows." Lion smiled lazily. "Wyatt saw to that personally. Plus—guess what? One of Wythe's aide-de-camps showed up in Maine just hours after we got Jillian out of there."

"So we were mere hours ahead of him. We were damned lucky we were able to move as fast as we did."

"Yes, we were."

Sin joined him at the table, taking the chair opposite him. "And now we're here, the *hardest* part of the plan, trying to guess what Wythe is going to do first and waiting for him to do it."

Lion grimaced. "Tell me about it. But I

think we're ready for anything. Wyatt and Nathan have got the other side of the island covered and we're maintaining an open line of communication with him at all times."

Sin nodded, his gaze straying back to Lily. "I don't think I ever heard Jonah's final decision. Did you convince him to stay put where he is?"

"Finally. It was harder than I thought it would be. He wanted to be in on the action in the worst way, but I got Jolie on my side." He chuckled. "Funny how a new bride can make a man rethink things, especially a new bride as lovely as Jolie."

Sin grinned. "Good for him."

"Yep, good for them both. And their honeymoon cabin is absolutely safe. It's not owned by the family and therefore not traceable to us, at least not in the amount of time Wythe has to act."

"Great. Jonah has more than earned the right to sit this one out."

"Good morning, Sin, Lion." Jacqueline appeared at their side and placed in the center of the table a tray laden with a carafe of coffee and a basket of freshly baked croissants and rolls.

"Good morning, Jacqueline."

"Good morning." Sin waited while she poured his coffee, then said, "Have you heard from Jillian this morning?"

She cast a critical eye over the table. "Not yet."

He glanced at his watch. "Give her another thirty minutes then check on her, would you?"

"Certainly. And I'll send Clay out with the melon and berries."

Lion waited until Jacqueline had strolled away before he spoke. "Jillian woke up before we expected her to yesterday, so we couldn't stop her before she got to you. Today she'll be watched."

Sin rubbed a finger against his temple. "Good. Just make sure the guards know she's to be treated like glass."

"Glass?"

Sin eyed him levelly. "I don't want her broken."

"She's Wythe's stepdaughter, Sin. Do you honestly think she could be?"

He did, though he couldn't have said why. "Just make sure, okay?"

Lion leaned back in his chair, his golden eyes filled with speculation. "No problem. But the drugs were the worst of it. Now that she's recovered from them, she'll be fine."

Sin nodded. "I hope so."

Lion watched him for a moment. "Anything you'd like to tell me?"

"Not particularly."

"Okay, then, I'll change the subject."

"Good idea."

Lion flashed him a knowing grin. "Abigail had some social engagements she didn't want to cancel, not even for our own personal little war, so Jo and Cale have moved in with her for the duration and Cale is working the security on that end. David flew out yesterday to be with Kylie so she doesn't have to skip any classes. Everyone else is either here or covered."

"Then we're set."

"Yeah, we're set." He paused. "Okay, Sin. Something is bothering the hell out of you. What is it?"

Sin shoved his stiffened fingers through his hair. "It's her—Jillian. I can't reconcile what I see when I look at her with the idea that she's Wythe's stepdaughter."

Lion shrugged. "Maybe it's because she's not his daughter by blood."

"I don't know that blood matters that much in her case. She was raised in *his* house, and after she was eleven, she was raised in *his* compound in the Middle East. No matter which way you cut it, that makes him her father."

Lion plucked a croissant from the basket and liberally spread it with jam. "I'll agree with that, but I'm still not sure what you expect to see."

"Someone who's hard, spoiled."

"And you don't?"

"No."

"Then what *do* you see?"

"Innocence and vulnerability."

Lion's forehead pleated. "Okay—so what? Let's say she's as pure as the driven snow. It changes nothing. Look, Sin, where she's concerned there's nothing for you to be worried about. As soon as this is all settled she'll be returned home, safe and sound."

"And angry as hell that we've captured her stepfather."

"I seem to remember us being pretty angry when our parents were killed." Lion spoke quietly. "And that was just one emotion we felt."

"She didn't plant that bomb."

"Yeah, well, that can't be helped. And why the hell are you beating yourself up over this, anyway? It's not like you. You know as well as I do that we've collected reams of information on Wythe, and in all of it, we've found only one thing, one person, outside his compound that he might risk his life for—Jillian."

"Jillian." Sin repeated the name, then rubbed his face. "I know, I know." He stood. "I'm going to join Lily on the beach. Keep me informed."

Jillian pushed open the French doors and strolled out onto the terrace. The warmth of the morning sun was gentle and the breeze was like silk against her skin. The beauty before her was endless, with colors that changed with the position of the sun, and flowers so glorious they seemed crafted by a mystical hand. True paradise, she reflected grimly. And nothing more than a gilded cage to her. She knew all about gilded cages and she hated them more than she could say.

Scanning the scene below her, she easily picked out the security people. One of them was standing just yards away from her, no doubt assigned to her. She'd been able to get to Sin twice without anyone stopping her. Obviously they planned to watch her more carefully from now on.

The faint sound of a little girl's laughter drifting up from the beach drew her attention. She saw Sin holding Lily's hand, bending down to her, and inspecting something she'd picked up from the sand.

He was a very powerful and ruthless man, determined to bring Steffan down at any cost, but yet he had all the time and gentleness in the world for his daughter. Any other time, any other circumstances, she'd be charmed.

She remembered last night and her sudden awareness of him as she'd looked at his lean, muscled body clad in nothing but a pair of silk boxers. There was an innate sensuality about him and a magnetism that had hit her squarely between the eyes.

But no more.

She had fallen for the lure of his jade-green eyes once; never again would she be around him without having her guard up.

Today she would watch and listen, and if there was any way for her to get off this island, she'd find it. And if there wasn't . . .

She shook her head, unable to force herself to face that problem just yet.

The faint sound of Lily's laughter came to her again and for the first time she wondered about Lily's mother. Sin had been alone in that big bed last night, yet she couldn't imagine that he was the type of man who could or would go without a woman for long.

"Miss Wythe?"

Startled, she wheeled to find Jacqueline standing in the doorway.

"I'm sorry to disturb you. I knocked on your door, and when you didn't answer, I came in to check on you."

Her lips twitched wryly. "It's all right, Jacqueline. I'm being held here against my will. You don't have to explain why you entered my room without permission. You can drop the pretense that I'm a guest."

Jacqueline's dark eyes were lovely and her voice was low and musical. "I worked for Mr.

Damaron's parents, and when they were killed, I stayed on to work for Mr. Damaron. Over the years I have taken care of many people who have come here, and I have treated everyone as an honored guest. I wouldn't know how to do my job any other way."

Jillian felt like a schoolgirl who had just been gently but firmly chastised. What a strange place this island was. An armed camp in paradise where everyone accepted her presence as normal.

"What would you like for breakfast?" Jacqueline asked. "Do you feel up to eating something more substantial this morning?"

Jillian sighed. She'd made up her food allergies on the spot, trying to give Sin a hard time and find out how far he'd go to accommodate her. If he were the one cooking her meals she would continue to give him trouble. But giving Jacqueline a hard time accomplished nothing. "Actually I'm starving. Anything you make will be fine with me."

"Good. I'll serve on the main terrace." She pointed to several levels below them where a long glass-top table and chairs were set. "And please, reflect on what else I can do to make your stay more comfortable. I understand you had to search for a pillow last night. If you think you might need anything else special perhaps we can take care of it today."

She gave a deferential nod of her head. "I'll see you in a few minutes with your breakfast."

So Sin had asked Jacqueline to find out her needs so that she wouldn't bother him again. Jillian smiled without humor. He should be so lucky.

She made her way down to the table. Sin had disappeared with Lily and so had the security guards that had been on the beach with them. She saw the man assigned to her, though. He had moved to within a discreet distance from her. His presence didn't bother her much. She had been giving Steffan's men the slip for many years now. She might not be able to get off the island today, but she was counting on being able to get away from one man for a few hours if she decided she needed to.

Looking back on the last six months, she supposed that her mistake had been to stay so long in one spot, working for Jimmy. The length of that employment was almost a record for her. But she'd gotten tired of moving so often and of never being able to hold on to friendships or put down roots. And she'd really been happy there; the town had been small enough and remote enough that she thought she might be able to remain undetected for a while. Her mistake.

"Good morning, Miss Wythe."

Jillian looked up to see the young man

who had helped serve dinner yesterday evening. "Good morning . . . Clay, is it?"

"That's right." He set down a pitcher filled with orange juice in the center of the table, along with another carafe of coffee. "I just squeezed the juice a few minutes ago," he said. "Our oranges are very sweet. I hope you like it."

She took another look at him. Seventeen, she guessed. Maybe eighteen. Big liquid dark eyes that didn't even try to hide the fact that he was smitten with her. She had never consciously flirted with anyone, much less a teenage boy, but the circumstances called for unusual measures. She gave him a charmfilled smile. "If you squeezed it, I'm sure I will like it. Thank you, Clay."

She saw a faint flush creep up his walnutcolored skin. "You're welcome. Well, uh—" He took several steps, reluctantly preparing to leave.

"Tell me something, Clay."

He immediately came back to her side. "Sure."

"Do you live here on the island?"

He nodded, a wide grin on his face. "All my life."

"Really? But what about school?"

"I've graduated from high school, and I've applied for college in the States. Mr. Damaron is going to pay my way as long as I keep my grades up. The Damarons make the same deal with all the kids on the island."

It wasn't really what she wanted to know, but she found the fact interesting nonetheless. "But where did you go to high school?"

"Oh, all the kids from here are flown daily to the next island over. They have excellent schools there."

"You were flown? By whom?"

He shrugged. "My uncle. Others. There are several pilots who live and work on the island."

Pilots. Airplanes. A possible way off the island. "Where's the airfield?"

"It's—"

"That will be all, Clay," Sin said smoothly. "Thank you."

"Sure, Mr. Damaron." He nodded awkwardly and hurried away.

Sin pulled out the chair next to hers and dropped down into it. "Shame on you, Jillian, for trying to dazzle information out of Clay. He's just a boy."

His dark good looks were startling against the jewel-colored backdrop of the island, and his eyes were the current color of the sea. Her heartbeat raced. Her body reacted to him in spite of her mind telling her she shouldn't. It was a new and unique experience for her and, under the circumstances, extremely unsettling. With effort, she managed to keep her voice calm. "Stacked beside what you're doing to me, it's nothing."

He nodded. "You've got me there, but do me a favor. If you want to know something, ask me. Don't bring my employees into this."

"Your employees *are* in it. They work for you. They live on this island, this island that you've in effect issued Steffan an invitation to. And you and I both know that if he comes, he won't come with gifts and friendship. Do you honestly think that there is anyone on this island who won't be affected?"

"Yes, as a matter of fact I do. But what I do or do not think about the matter is not the issue here. Getting Clay to fall for you will do you *zero* good and will only cause a problem for Jacqueline when she has to nurse his broken heart."

"There's no way I would break Clay's heart."

He smiled. "You could do it in a snap, Jillian, so ask *me* what it is you want to know. I have the answers."

She had thought that very thing when she was going in and out of consciousness, when her only knowledge of him had been his eyes. "You're very protective of Clay and Jacqueline."

"People who show me loyalty receive loyalty in return."

"And what do you do about people who are disloyal?"

He smiled, showing white even teeth. "I feed them to the sharks in the bay."

There wasn't a doubt in her mind that he would be capable of doing just that, especially if his family were involved. Strangely, though, she didn't believe that he had ever done it. She also didn't believe there were too many people who would dare to be disloyal to him.

Wearing a forest-green, short-sleeve knit shirt paired with taupe slacks, he sat with the ankle of one leg resting on the knee of the other. Grains of sand clung to the bottom of the slacks, and its material stretched tautly over his thighs. She was finding that looking at any part of him was seductive.

She pushed herself back to reality. "So, you want me to ask you my questions?"

"That's right."

"But will you give me the *right* answers?"

"Yes. I'll even give you a map of the island, if you want. But, Jillian, you're not going to get away."

His tone was calm and assured, and he was very positive. And because he was, the all-too-familiar panic began to rise in her. "I *can't* stay here."

"Why not? It's not like you're being kept in some dank cell, being fed a diet of bread and water."

Her hand balled into a fist on the table. "Do you honestly think it makes it any less wrong to keep me here because I'm not being kept under those conditions?"

Intensity glittered in his eyes. "There's nothing right about any of this, Jillian. But then there is very little about life that's right. However, the fact that you've got a bed to sleep in instead of a cot, and anything you want to eat rather than bread and water, certainly should make it more pleasant for you."

Her nerves crawled. "Pleasant? You think this should be *pleasant* for me?"

"I told you yesterday. It's up to you."

"Damn you, Sin. You can't play God with people's lives like this. I have a *job*. Jimmy—" She touched her forehead in sudden realization. "Lord, what in the world must he think?"

"He thinks that you had to leave quickly because you were notified that your mother is very ill."

"Why," she said slowly, "does he think that?"

"Because he got a note signed by you, telling him just exactly that."

She stared at him. "You thought of everything, didn't you?"

"I tried."

"And it doesn't matter to you that I have

nothing to do with what's between you and Steffan? That I'm innocent?"

"My parents were also innocent. So were my aunts and uncles."

She should have known that there would be no reasoning with him. The man was stone. It would take a chisel and hammer to reach his heart, *if* he even had one.

"I'm sorry, Jillian."

His apology completely threw her. In fact she barely managed to keep her mouth from dropping open. "For what?"

"For disrupting your life."

She didn't have to scramble to regroup. She knew exactly what she wanted to say. "Then you'll let me go? You'll fly me back to Maine?"

"As soon as Wythe shows up."

"Damn you, Sin."

"Nothing's changed, Jillian. I deeply regret that you've had to be put in the middle, but the fact remains it was the only way."

"The only way to get what *you* want, regardless of what it does to me."

"I'm sorry."

Such a complicated man, she thought. And so infuriating. "It's not going to work, you know. Steffan won't come."

"You mean, you *hope* he won't."

Suddenly she became aware of a painful lump in her throat and the cold dampness of her palms. She was trying so hard not to be afraid. There were times when she thought she was beginning to succeed. But then the fear would come rushing back, taking her unawares, and reminding her how very afraid she really was. "You're right. I hope he won't. But if he does, and I'm here, he'll get me. And you will have accomplished nothing. Nothing."

He nodded thoughtfully. "I can understand why you believe Wythe will be successful. You know your stepfather's capabilities, and you don't know mine. However, I can assure you, there's no way I'll allow myself to fail in this matter."

She shook her head, frustrated beyond belief. "Try to understand. For years Steffan has been putting money into the coffers of the country where he lives. He is very much in favor with their government. He can tap into any of their resources, up to and including the military."

"So you know that, huh?"

She blinked in surprise. "Are you saying you know it too?"

"Yes. It's why we chose to lure him to us. It wouldn't be impossible to get him out of that country, but it would be very, very difficult and involve taking a great many unnecessary risks."

"You know the power he has, and you're

still going up against him? Have you lost your mind?"

A smile touched his lips. "As I said, you don't know my capabilities. But you will . . . you will."

She shifted uncomfortably. "Well, I do know part of what you're capable of. I'm here because of it."

"Yes, you are." Sin's tone was as soft as his gaze as it rested on her. Her hair glinted in the sunlight, the silky strands looking as if they had been tossed rather than combed. And her gray eyes were so clear they reflected the colors around her. She was breathtakingly lovely, and something about her made him want to take care of her, to protect her. Even more unfathomable, he wanted to ask her to understand why he was doing what he was doing.

But it wasn't appropriate, and it would be too much to ask. Besides, as Lion had said, she would soon be out of their lives. "Tell me something, Jillian. If you didn't know about Wythe being responsible for the bombing of my family's plane, then what reason did he give you and your mother for moving to the Middle East?"

Her eyes widened. "Are you saying the bomb was why he moved us?"

"That's what I'm saying. My cousins and I were young at the time and no real threat to him. However, he had to know that sooner or later we'd come after him, or that someone would turn up the evidence to convict him. The country he chose has no extradition treaty with the United States."

"I don't know what he told my mother, but he told me that he would be better able to take care of her there."

"Take care of her?"

"Doctors, medicines, that sort of thing."

"And you believed him?"

"I was eleven years old. I had no choice."

"Choice? That's an interesting way to put it. I would have thought you'd say that it never entered your mind to question him."

"Put it any way you like, Sin," she said, a thread of irritation in her voice. "What difference does it make?"

"I'm not sure."

"It makes *no* difference."

"Okay." The last thing he wanted to do was argue with her and put any more strain between them. "So even back then, your mother wasn't well?"

"Not really, no."

"And has Wythe taken good care of your mother, as he said he would?"

"He has taken excellent care of my mother."

"I suppose it's one of the reasons why you

find it so hard to believe that he did the horrendous thing I say he did."

Jillian wasn't certain how to respond to him. He would probably be very surprised at the things she knew Steffan to be capable of, but to think that he, or anyone for that matter, could be responsible for killing almost an entire family was almost unimaginable. On the other hand, for Sin and his family to take the radical steps they had, she had to consider that they had undeniable proof against Steffan.

Jacqueline's appearance on the terrace saved her from having to respond. Beside her, Clay pushed a food cart.

Sin surveyed the waffles, bacon, rolls, and fresh fruit with a critical eye. "Did you remember about Jillian's egg allergy?" he asked Jacqueline.

"Yes, I did."

"Don't waffles have eggs in them?"

Jacqueline's response was serene. "These don't."

He wasn't aware she had made up the allergy to eggs, Jillian thought, but she was still surprised that he would make such a big point of it. "Thank you, Jacqueline. Clay."

Clay flashed her a quick grin, which she returned, despite Sin's look of displeasure. Truly hungry, she picked up her fork and began to eat.

Sin waited until Jacqueline and Clay had left before speaking. "Did Jacqueline speak with you this morning about any special needs you might have?"

"Yes, she did—your idea, I'm guessing."

"That's right."

"Forgive me if I'm not touched by your concern for me. For one thing, it's obvious you don't want to be bothered by me. For another, it's also obvious that Steffan won't come to rescue me if I've died because I ate eggs. Or for any other reason, for that matter."

"For God's sake, Jillian. Has it occurred to you that I don't have to do any of the things I've done to ensure your comfort? That I could simply lock you in a room and send food in periodically?"

No, it hadn't occurred to her. She'd been too busy trying to cope with the fact that she was being held hostage and trying to figure out what she could do about it. "Do you expect me to thank you for being humane?"

"No," he said. "I guess that would be expecting too much."

There was a weariness in his tone that she hadn't heard before and a hint of disappointment. And to her surprise, she felt a surge of guilt. Neat trick, she thought wryly. How in the world had he done it?

She waited for him to say something else,

but he didn't. And she received her second surprise. She *wanted* him to talk to her. "Okay, Sin, tell me about the island."

"Anything in particular?"

"Yes. Tell me how I can get off it."

Humor touched his lips. "There are two ways on and off this island—you can go by sea or you can go by air. The airfield is situated at the highest point of the island and is big enough to land small jets. However, no one on this island will fly you anywhere, not even two feet down the runway. As for the sea, we currently have a fleet of boats of various sizes and types, but there is no way you'd be able to even get near any of them. If they're not in use, they're being heavily guarded."

"Why?" Sarcasm laced the question. "Are there people on this island besides me who want to get off?"

"No, but very soon there are going to be people trying to get on."

A chill shuddered through her. She'd love to assure Sin that she would escape despite all his security, because no matter what Steffan had done, she would not be used in this fashion. But her assurances would not only be hollow, they would fall on deaf ears. She'd fought most of her life not to be a captive and now she was one and there didn't seem to be anything she could do about it.

She was caught between two powerful

men, one who had kidnapped her to use her as bait and the other who was responsible for blowing a planeload of people out of the sky. If she were to gauge the weight of the sins committed, Steffan would certainly be the winner.

But none of that changed the fact that the control of her life had been taken out of her hands, however temporarily. And because it had, she was having to fight a suffocating panic. It was nothing she could explain or even rationalize. The panic just was. And she didn't know what she was going to do about it.

FIVE

After breakfast, Jillian retreated to her room, but she was too restless to sit still for long. She discovered a pile of recently published magazines, but no article could hold her. She was certainly in no mood to read about the life of any celebrity; likewise she could have cared less about one-hundred-and-one-new-and-creative ways to prepare ground meat. She also found a television set tucked behind cabinet doors, along with a stack of videotapes and a VCR. With a roll of her eyes she turned away.

She paced the length of the bedroom and back again. It was a large, luxurious room, but once again she had to compare her surroundings to a gilded cage that Sin Damaron had put her in. Her skin felt too tight, her nerves too raw. Each breath she drew was an effort, until finally she didn't feel there was one more breath of oxygen left for her to breathe.

Abruptly she went out onto the terrace. There, at least, the ever-present trade winds made it *seem* as if there was air.

For as long as she could remember, she'd been afraid of being in a place she couldn't get out of. It was a form of claustrophobia that had nothing to do with the size of the place where she was, but rather an intense need for freedom, a need to be able to come and go as she wished, a need to be able to *see* a way out.

In this case, she couldn't. She could leave the room, but she couldn't leave the island. All she could do was wait for Steffan to come and get her, a situation she found utterly intolerable and terrifying.

She headed toward the beach, vaguely aware of a guard trailing her from a distance. Today his constant presence was like a mosquito she longed to swat.

She was also aware of men with silver streaks in their hair coming and going from the house, talking in groups of two or three on the terrace, apparently their own exotic tribe. She did her best to shut them out of her mind.

Reaching the sand, she kicked off her shoes and proceeded to the water's edge. After rolling up her jeans to just below her knee, she waded into water as warm as a bath and clear enough to see to the sandy bottom.

It seemed impossible that anything bad could happen amid such beauty, she reflected. But she could see why Sin and his family had chosen the island on which to confront Steffan. Even though it would be impossible to guard every inch of it, it could certainly be defended more easily than most pieces of land. Plus, the isolation of the island ensured that there would be no interference from any agency of law. Perhaps the Damarons would be a match for Steffan, after all. It seemed they made their own laws. It was a startling thought to her.

She waded from the water and dropped onto the white sand, finer than sugar and warm from the sun. Turquoise waves rolled toward her and spilled onto the shore in lacy patterns that reached almost to her bare toes. Over her, seagulls soared against a china-blue sky. The beauty was unreal, the violence that threatened very real.

She leaned back on her elbows and stretched her long legs out in front of her and tried one more time to confront what Sin had told her. *If* Steffan had killed Sin's parents, along with his aunts and uncles, she could understand why Sin had kidnapped her. She hated more than she could say the fact that he had taken her against her will, but on some level she now understood why he had done it. And she even had to agree with him that Steffan might—in fact, he probably would—come out of exile to try to rescue her.

Blowing out a long breath of frustration, she lowered herself to the sand until she was lying full length on it. The sun warmed her skin and soothed her nerves. Above her, puffy, cotton-white clouds drifted. When she had been a child she had been able to spend long hours trying to find animal shapes in the clouds. But today there was no diverting her thoughts with the game. It was impossible to focus on anything so trivial when there was so much at stake.

Slowly her lids closed, shutting out the clouds and the sky. But to her chagrin, a pair of jade-green eyes appeared in her mind, the same pair of green eyes that had gotten her in this trouble in the first place. And ever since that day in Maine, those same eyes and the man who possessed them had been arousing strong and uncommon emotions in her. . . .

Frustration.

Anger.

Curiosity.

There was even a certain amount of fascination.

The first time she'd seen him, he'd been sitting on the beach, staring out at the coming storm as if he were not just unafraid, but *accustomed* to storms.

Well, by luring Steffan from his hiding place, he had certainly conjured up one hell of a storm, and when it came, it would hit the peaceful island with an unimaginable force. Indeed, the coming storm would leave no one untouched. Not Sin and his family and certainly not her.

"Shhh, Daddy. She's sleepin'."

She heard Lily's voice, and then Sin's.

"Then why don't we leave her alone, baby. She may need to rest."

"But I want to ask her—"

"It's okay." Jillian sat up and smoothed her hair away from her face. If Sin actually thought she could get some rest while the two of them stood over her, talking about her, he was crazy. "Hi, Lily."

Lily looked adorable in a pale green pinafore with white sandals on her feet and a matching green bow tying up her curly hair. She retreated behind one of her daddy's legs and peered around at her. "Hi."

In many ways, Lily's green eyes were as enchanting as her father's, she thought. But she found it a lot easier to look into Lily's eyes than she did Sin's. "Was there something you wanted, Lily?"

The little girl nodded. With a gentle hand against her back, Sin urged her from behind him. "Come on, Lily. Now's not the time to be bashful. Ask her."

Still hanging on to her father's leg, Lily stared at her for a moment, then broke into an adorable grin. "Daddy and I are having a tea party. Could you come?"

"A tea party?" True, the island was in the lull before the storm, but she was still taken aback by the incongruity of such an innocent and sweet idea.

Lily nodded. "Daddy said you wouldn't have time, but you're just sleepin', so you'd have time, wouldn't you?"

So he'd given her a way out. Had he been thinking of himself or of her? she wondered. "A tea party," she said again, just to make sure she hadn't misunderstood. Lily nodded.

Sin spoke up. "I promised Lily yesterday evening that today we'd do something special together and she chose a tea party."

Jillian remembered. He'd been trying to get Lily to go back to bed. She stood, tired of having to crane her neck to see him, and brushed the sand off her jeans. "Where are you having your tea party, Lily?"

The little girl pointed back up the slope toward the house, where a quilt had been spread over the grass.

"I explained to Lily you might have something else to do," Sin said, drawing her attention back to him.

Speculation glinted in his eyes, along with something else she couldn't interpret. Whatever it was, she was sure he didn't want her to come. "As it happens, I don't have anything to do, Lily. I'd love to come to your tea party."

Lily's face lit up. "Yeah! Yeah!" She tugged on her daddy's hand. "Let's go!"

"Thank you for saying you'd come," Sin murmured to her as the three of them fell into step, side by side.

Well, she thought wryly, that blew her theory that he didn't want her with them, which left her to wonder at her reasons for accepting. "Lily seemed to want me, and there really wasn't any reason to disappoint her." The little girl skipped alongside her father, her hand tucked trustingly in his, without a care in the world. Jillian envied her.

"Still, it was very nice of you. Under the circumstances, I wouldn't have been surprised if you'd said no."

"Under the circumstances?" Her lips twitched with humor. "You do have a way of understating things."

The humor caught him off guard, and at that moment Lily broke away to run on ahead to the blanket. "I'm trying to keep her life as normal as possible."

"Every little girl should have a chance for a carefree childhood, no matter . . ."

Now it was his turn for his lips to twitch. "No matter who her father is?"

"No matter who or what," she said flatly.

An oversized blanket, populated with several dolls in different sizes and shapes, lay beneath a jacaranda tree that dripped with lovely blue flowers.

"Please, sit down," Lily said in her best four-year-old hostess tone. "These are my babies." She pointed to several dolls propped up against one another.

Jillian did as she was bid. "So I see. They're very pretty."

"Thank you." Lily picked each one up by turn and introduced them to her. "This is Maisie, this is Veronica, this is Heidi, and this is Annabel."

Jillian solemnly inclined her head. "It's a pleasure meeting you, Maisie, Veronica, Heidi, and Annabel."

"They like you."

"Well, I like them too."

With a beaming smile, Lily busied herself with the child-size tea set in the middle of the blanket.

Sin dropped down beside Jillian. Since

Lily, her dolls, and the tea set were taking up most of the blanket it was really the only place left for him, yet Jillian got the puzzling impression that he would have sat beside her anyway.

"Daddy! You knocked the teacup over!"

"Sorry, baby."

The look he gave Jillian shared his amusement with her and struck her as curiously intimate—under the circumstances. The phrase came back to her. An understatement, yes. In fact, the circumstances called for strong, powerful reactions. But then, this was a decidedly gentle moment, she thought, watching as Lily set about pouring imaginary tea into teeny cups for her dolls. In her experience, gentle moments were to be cherished.

Then Sin broke the spell. "After today, I'd appreciate it if you would stay closer to the house."

"You are so strange," Jillian said, shaking her head, bemused more than angry. "You'd *appreciate* it? You make it sound as if I have choice."

Sin shot a glance at Lily to make sure she was too busy with her dolls to pay attention to the grown-ups. "We both know you don't, but I see no point in being any more heavy-handed than I've already had to be."

"And I should be grateful for these little courtesies?"

"Actually, if I were you, I'd be mad as hell."

"I'm furious."

Her words were whispered and drew his gaze to her lips. They were soft and lush and the urge to taste them was almost overwhelming. But he'd forced her to come to the island against her will; he couldn't force her to do anything else. All he could do was try to reassure her. "I can understand that. I hope, though, you're not afraid."

The concern in his expression puzzled her. "Afraid?"

"There's no reason to be afraid, Jillian. You won't be hurt."

There were different degrees and kinds of hurt, as she well knew, but a man like Sin would never understand that. "There's no way you can guarantee that." She kept her voice deliberately low and even, in tacit agreement with him that Lily shouldn't be upset.

"Oh, but I can."

"You're not God."

He smiled and her breath caught at the unexpected charm of it.

"Believe it or not, I know that, but as I said, you will not be hurt."

She shook her head, unable to believe him and unwilling to explain her fears. "Have you heard from Steffan?"

He hesitated. "Not directly, but there's definite activity in and around his compound, *new* activity."

"You've got people close enough to his compound to be able to tell that?"

"Yes."

She was intimately familiar with Steffan's power and now she was becoming familiar with Sin's. Men of power wearied her, repelled her, under certain circumstances even frightened her, because men of power usually did exactly what they wanted without thought to anyone else. Sin said he didn't think he was God, but his actions with regard to her belied his words. "So you think Steffan will be coming soon?"

"Yes, I do."

"And then what will happen?"

With a look at Lily, who was singing to herself, he again hesitated. "I only know two things for sure: He won't give himself up, and he will try to get you out of here."

Unfortunately and amazingly, she considered his assessment dead on. "How do you know so much about him?"

"I've had a person on the inside of his camp for some time."

Astounding, she thought, since she knew how carefully Steffan screened those around him. Also troubling. For the first time it occurred to her to wonder at the *extent* of Sin's knowledge. She had spent most of her adult life trying every way she could think of to guard her privacy, and now this man was in a position to know most, if not everything, about her.

"It is well known that he adores his step-daughter. I've been told there are picture of you in every room, and every time you come home he makes a huge deal out of it, pushing the people who work for him to make sure everything is perfect for you."

Lily saved her from having to answer. "Here," she said, handing her a small cup and saucer filled with real tea. "And see these cakes? I helped Jacqueline make them."

Jillian dutifully took a little cake. "How wonderful, Lily. I'm very impressed."

The little girl giggled. "I'm a good cook. Jacqueline says so. Here, Daddy." She handed him a cake.

"Thank you, baby."

Lily returned her attention to her dolls. "Here, Maisie." She held an empty cup up to the doll's painted lips.

"Do you really think you're a match for Steffan?" Jillian asked Sin beneath her breath.

"I'm sorry, but yes, I do."

Unsure whether she believed him or not, she took a bite of the cake so that she wouldn't hurt Lily's feelings. "This is very good, Lily."

"Thank you." Suddenly Lily popped to her feet. "I forgot the honey for the tea! I'll be right back."

Jillian's gaze followed her as she ran off toward the house. "She's a wonderful little girl."

"Thank you," Sin said. "I think so."

With Lily gone, along with the need to watch their words and their tone, an awkward silence fell between them. Minutes passed. Brightly colored birds flitted in the trees. Occasionally she would hear the sound of men talking or the distant motor of a boat as it cruised just offshore. And the urge to ask him one particular question grew. But she put it off and asked another instead.

With a gesture to his hair, she said, "I've seen a lot of people on the island with silver streaks in their hair. And you have one and so do Lion and Lily."

A slight smile touched his lips. "That's because they're Damarons and, of course, so am I. Every Damaron by blood has the streak."

"I figured it was hereditary, but it's unusual for *everyone* in your family to have inherited it."

"For better or for worse, it's our mark."

"I gather you and your family are very well known?"

"More than any of us likes."

She nodded. "I guess I should know that, but I rarely saw an American paper when I was growing up. Now I rarely have time to do more than keep up on current events."

"Feel yourself blessed. There's a lot of trash and nonsense that gets printed every day."

"I suppose." Another silence fell between them. "Where . . ." She hesitated, strangely reluctant to know the answer to the real question she wanted to ask. In the end, though, the urge to know won out. "Where is your wife?"

"I'm not married."

Her head whipped around. "You're divorced from Lily's mother?"

"We were never married."

"But I don't understand. Where is Lily's mother? Why isn't she here with her daughter?" The thought flashed through her mind that with Sin's power, he might have wrested custody of Lily away from the unknown mother.

"Lily's mother is dead."

She drew in a quick breath. "I'm sorry."

He didn't answer, but his expression was as hard as she had ever seen it.

"So you've raised her all by yourself." It wasn't really a question. Even though she'd known him only a short time, it was obvious to her that Sin would not let anyone else raise a child of his.

"Of course," he said.

Veronica toppled over. Automatically he reached out to straighten the doll, and while he was at it he tugged her little white eyelet petticoat into place.

Such a simple thing for him to do, she reflected. An incredibly sweet thing, and he did it without thought. Yet she knew him to be a ruthless man who had an army of cold-eyed men working for him, ready to help him conduct his own private war.

"Daddy!" Lily came running back toward them.

As he drew his hand away from the doll, he accidentally brushed Jillian's arm, burning her with the brief contact. She looked down at her arm, shocked at the feeling of heat that lingered there still.

"I got the honey." Lily sounded out of breath as she collapsed onto the blanket and held up the container to show them.

"Thank you for going to get that," Jillian said, and as unobtrusively as possible placed her hand on her arm where her skin still tingled.

"You're welcome." Lily cast a hostesslike look at them both. "Have you been drinking your tea?"

Sin smiled at his daughter. "Yes, ma'am."

"And did you eat my cake?"

"If I eat any more, I'll be so heavy, I won't be able to get up."

She giggled. "Silly, Daddy."

The gaze he rested on his daughter was incredibly gentle, yet Jillian had seen those same eyes hard as stone. But he didn't put on an act where his daughter was concerned, that much she was very sure of. And when it came to Lily, he didn't have a self-conscious bone in his body. He was too confident and self-possessed to be concerned that she would see his softness with Lily as a weakness.

"Daddy?"

"What, baby?"

"Hold Heidi. She's unhappy."

His demeanor softened. "I'm so sorry to hear that." He took the doll and sat her in his lap. "Heidi, don't be unhappy. Lily's tea is very good." He reached for one of the empty teacups and held it to the doll's mouth.

Lily dissolved into giggles, and Jillian marveled at the complexity of the man called Sin. His eyes were steely as he spoke of the woman who had born him a child, yet he clearly doted on that very child. And he was unafraid to go up against a man who was perfectly capable of bringing the weapons and armies of an entire country against him.

"Did you know I have a dog?" Lily asked her, drawing her attention back to her.

"No, I didn't."

Lily nodded, her eyes big with the importance of what she was saying. "His name is Kirby, but he had to stay home in New York."

"Oh, I see." A child's chatter could be relaxing, she thought. Undemanding.

"Do you have a little girl?" Lily asked her unexpectedly.

"No, I don't," she said, quickly recovering. She should have known better than to relax around *either* Damaron.

"Do you have a little boy?"

"No. I don't have any children."

Lily regarded her solemnly, then handed her one of her dolls. "You can have Annabel for a while."

"Have? Oh, no, I couldn't take one of your dolls."

"It's okay. You can keep her while you're here. She'll help you not be afraid."

"Afraid?"

Lily nodded. "Daddy said you shouldn't be afraid."

Startled, she looked at Sin, who was regarding his daughter thoughtfully. Lily had heard at least part of what they were talking about. She reached out and caressed Lily's soft cheek. "Don't you worry about me, okay, sweetheart? I'll be fine."

Lily nodded with a grave wisdom that seemed beyond her years. "Okay, but Annabel will keep you company."

"Thank you." It was all she could think to say. "And anytime you want her back, let me know."

"Okay."

Jillian looked down at the doll in her lap. "You know what, Lily? I used to have a doll very much like Annabel."

"Really?"

"Yes." The doll had had a soft, huggable body and big brown eyes. She couldn't remember the name, but she did recall that it seemed to understand everything that she was feeling. "I guess every little girl needs a doll like Annabel."

With that lack of self-consciousness she found so amazing, Sin reached for his daughter and pulled her into his arms.

"And every daddy needs a Lily to hug," he said with mock gruffness as he held her tight and kissed the nape of her sweet neck. "Except no one but me has the *real* Lily."

"Da-ddy!" Lily squealed with delight.

Jillian elected to eat dinner alone that night. She badly needed a respite from the Damarons. Sin was too likable when he was with his daughter, too gentle and caring. And Lily was too knowing. Between the two of them, they left her feeling extremely vulnerable.

And Sin alone, without his daughter, was way too disturbing.

Dark and brooding, he presented to her a formidable problem. She was in the worst position of her life and she needed to do something about it. No matter what Sin said about the invulnerability of the island, she should be trying to figure out how to escape. Yet the thing uppermost in her mind at the moment was to learn more about him and the woman he had made a baby with.

"Foolish, Jillian," she said aloud. "Very foolish."

A knock sounded at the door and she went to answer it.

"Good evening, Miss Wythe." Clay rolled a food cart into the room. "Where would you like your dinner set up?"

"Uh, anywhere, I guess." She wasn't accustomed to being waited on. In fact she would have much preferred to pop into the kitchen and make herself a sandwich. But from her years of working in restaurants, plus her experience with Steffan's household, she knew cooks could be positively territorial, and she had no wish to raise Jacqueline's ire. "And please, call me Jillian."

He grinned, pure pleasure written all over him. "Okay, Jillian." He pulled a table in front of the open French doors and began to set up the dinner there, all the while casting surreptitious glances at her.

There was something fresh and unspoiled about Clay, compared with American teenagers, she reflected.

"I hope you're not too unhappy," he said, a pink tinge creeping up his neck.

"I'm fine, Clay." There was no point in venting her anger on Clay. He was an innocent party in all of this, just as she was.

He straightened and looked at her, his expression earnest. "Please don't think too harshly of Mr. Damaron."

She sighed at his determination to talk to her about her situation. "Your Mr. Damaron kidnapped me, Clay. You can't expect me to be happy about that."

"But he had an excellent reason."

"An excellent reason for *him*, Clay, not for me."

"But you can have a very nice stay here. You can swim, fish, hike—"

"Fish?" she asked with sudden interest. "You mean out in a boat on the water?"

"No," he said regretfully. "Not until Mr. Wythe has been captured, but there is a pier where I go a lot."

She shook her head, disappointed. "No, thanks." For a brief moment she'd thought she'd seen a way off the island.

"But—"

"Clay, don't worry about me. I told you, I'm fine."

"Okay, but if you change your mind about going fishing—"

"I'll let you know. Thank you."

They were going to kill her with kindness, she thought wryly. She debated with herself as she watched him turn back to his duties. She had no business asking him the question that she so sorely wanted to ask him. On the other hand, she was being held on the island against her will. Why should she be bothered by good manners? And where was the harm in a little idle curiosity? "You've lived here all your life, Clay. Did you ever meet Lily's mother?"

The smile faded from his face as he looked at her. "You shouldn't believe those tabloids."

"What tabloids?"

"Those tabloids that talk about scandals all the time. They didn't tell it like it really was with Mr. Damaron."

"You mean the tabloids actually *wrote* about Sin?"

"Yes."

In her experience, tabloids wrote about

people who were well-known, larger than life,
and certainly outside her experience. But then
again, Sin *was* outside her experience.

Clay was obviously as eager as a puppy
dog to talk to her, and equally pleased that he
could defend his hero. "They said it was his
fault that she killed herself, but it wasn't."

Her hand flew to her heart. "Lily's
mother *killed* herself?"

"Everyone blamed him, but Aunt Jacqueline said he sure didn't lead her to the bridge
and push her off." He went back to laying out
her dinner.

Well, she'd had to ask. "No, I wouldn't
imagine he did."

"I hope you like dinner. Aunt Jacqueline
said to tell you she didn't use one egg. And
it's chicken, not seafood."

"Tell her thank you. So, what happened?
Why did everyone blame Mr. Damaron?"

"She left a note that said he had ruined
her life and she couldn't go on. The tabloids
printed the note, but they shouldn't have. Mr.
Damaron is an honorable man."

She could argue with him about his defini-
tion of honorable in regard to Sin, but she'd
never convince Clay that she was right. She
sat down on the edge of the bed. "So why do
you think her suicide *wasn't* his fault?"

"Because it wasn't. Aunt Jacqueline said

that Mr. Damaron told Lily's mother that he didn't love her and that he wouldn't marry her, but that he'd take care of her. He was very up-front with her."

She tried to put herself in the shoes of the unknown woman, carrying Sin's child. If the woman had loved Sin, then Jillian could understand why she would have been devastated that he didn't love her in return. On the other hand, she strongly believed that killing oneself was never an answer to anything. "You sound so sure."

He straightened away from the table. "I am. Mr. Damaron is a wonderful man. He wouldn't have been deceitful with any woman."

Funny, but she could believe that. Sin had never pulled any punches with her.

"Aunt Jacqueline said that the facts were actually there in the tabloid, just buried beneath the trash. Aunt Jacqueline said Lily's mother was a rich, neurotic woman who went after Mr. Damaron with every trick in the book."

"Trick?"

"She tried to manipulate him."

Manipulating Sin would not be easy, she thought. If it could be done at all. Still . . . "She must have succeeded to a certain extent. She got pregnant."

"Against his wishes."

"She couldn't have done it by herself."

Clay blushed and Jillian realized she'd taken the conversation much further than idle curiosity.

"Your dinner is ready, Jillian."

"Oh—thanks, Clay."

"Sure. When you're through, just ring and I'll come pick it up. And listen. . . ."

"Yes?"

He shook his head. "Nothing, I guess. Just . . . anytime you want to talk, let me know. And if you want anything—"

"I'll call. Thank you."

Clay was a nice young man, she thought, after he'd left. But she never should have encouraged him to talk about Sin and Lily's mother as she had. She had no excuse. Even though the people she had met on this island had a way of making her like them, feel at ease with them, she still had no excuse.

Except she couldn't help but be curious about Sin. She frowned at herself. His daughter was way too adorable and he himself was much too compelling. To make it worse, his cause was even just.

But his methods were deplorable, and the sooner she was able to leave this place, these people—*him*—the better off she'd be.

Her gaze went to Annabel, propped up against a pillow on her bed. If only things were as simple as Lily thought they were. If only she could be comforted by a doll, or be reassured by Sin when he told her she had nothing to be afraid of.

But he didn't understand. None of them did. She did, though, and she *was* afraid.

SIX

There was no light.

Jillian sat straight up in bed, her heart pounding. Frantically she reached out for the bedside lamp and turned the switch. No light. Only darkness and black sinister shapes, waiting for her. Oh, Lord.

She had to get to the light.

She bolted from the bed and raced for the door. The hallway was lit, but her heartbeat refused to slow. Waking in the dark terrorized her. She couldn't think. She only knew that the dark held evil. And pain.

She *hated* the dark. It was why she fought sleep so hard. It was why she always slept with the light on.

She glanced back into the bedroom. Its thick silent darkness loomed menacingly.

She wheeled and headed for the double

doors at the end of the hallway; as quietly as possible she slipped inside.

Sin's bedroom was dark, but she could hear his deep, even breathing, feel the warmth from his body, and she drew an easier breath, already beginning to feel better. The thought of the gun he kept at his bedside entered her mind only fleetingly. In comparison with waking to a darkened room, a gun held no terror. She went straight to his bed and climbed up on it.

The bedside lamp was switched on, flooding the bed and the small area around it with illumination, and Sin sat up in bed. "Jillian? What—"

"My light, it went out. There's no light. None. It went out."

He rubbed his eyes, then reached for the heavy gold watch on the bedside table. "It's three A.M., Jillian. What are you doing up?"

"I told you—my light went out." She wrapped her arms around her waist, hugging herself tightly. "I left it on when I went to sleep—I always do—but when I woke up it was dark."

He took a closer look at her. She was wearing a cream cotton sleep shift, her arms and shoulders were bare, the swell of her breast tantalizing above the low neckline. But her skin was ashen and her eyes were dark with fear. "Which light are you talking about?"

"My bedside light." She pointed to the lamp he had turned on. "Like that one."

"The bulb burned out?"

"I guess." She hugged herself tighter. Lightbulbs burned out—logically she understood that. But logic played no part in what she was feeling, in the unshakable childhood fear that someone could have crept into her room while she slept and turned the light out, then lurked—waiting, planning, watching.

"And so you came in here to tell me?" he asked, trying to understand.

"Yes."

It was apparent that something other than the obvious was going on with her, he reflected grimly. To make matters worse she was looking at him as Lily sometimes did, as if she were waiting for him to give her an answer or solve a problem. If she had been Lily he would know exactly how to comfort her, but she wasn't a child and he sure as hell didn't feel fatherly toward her. She was an extremely desirable woman who, for whatever reason, happened to be very vulnerable at the moment, and his body was reacting to her, pulsing with desire—totally *inappropriate* desire. He edged closer to her and reached out to touch her cheek and told himself it was not just an excuse to touch her, but rather a way to comfort her. Right, he thought ruefully. "I'll get you a new bulb—okay?"

"Okay."

"Okay." Except he couldn't make himself move away from her, not when she looked as if she might break, not when she looked so soft and damnably tempting, her skin gleaming with the luster of silk in the lamplight, her hair making his fingers itch to comb through it, to create more disorder and tangled loveliness. "Are you afraid of the dark, Jillian?"

Her first impulse was to deny it, but then almost immediately she realized how silly it would be to deny something so obvious. Her heartbeat was slowing, her fear receding. But she still wasn't ready to go back to the vast emptiness of her room and the darkness that most certainly would be lingering. "Yes," she said reluctantly. "I am when I sleep."

"So you're used to sleeping with something brighter than a normal night-light?"

Absently she brushed strands of hair from her forehead that immediately slipped back. "I always leave the lamp on."

Fascinated by her hair, by her, he tried his luck with the same portion of her hair, pushing at the strands, then watching them slide back. "Is there some particular reason for your fear?"

His touch on her brow sent a heated shiver through her. She clasped her hands together in her lap and gazed down at them. She couldn't explain her fear to him any more than she could explain to herself why she had come to him. "Look, I'm sorry. I know how foolish this all must seem to you."

"Don't apologize. None of us can help the things we're afraid of."

"No, I suppose not." He was being unexpectedly understanding, but she couldn't imagine that he would have fears.

"But it's not so surprising," he said. "You're in a strange place, in a very strained situation."

She wavered between feeling very comfortable on his bed and extremely awkward. At the moment awkwardness ruled. But then she supposed there were no rules of etiquette that covered their situation. His sheets were smooth and soft and smelled of him. The way he was sitting caused his silk boxers to stretch taut against him, giving her more than a hint of his masculinity. Her mouth, she noticed, was extremely dry. "You know, now that I think about it, I guess I should have called Jacqueline."

His lips curved into a knowing smile. "Now, why would you want to do that? If you had, I might have gotten a full night's sleep."

So he had seen through her actions the night before, she reflected ruefully, and he had gone along with her anyway, helping her look for exactly the right pillow. Yet more proof that he was no ordinary man.

"Besides," he added, still smiling, "my room is closer to yours than Jacqueline's."

She nodded, feeling doubly foolish. Last night she had deliberately set out to disturb his sleep and he had responded with forbearance. And here they were again, in the middle of the night, both of them wearing very little. Unwittingly and unthinkingly she had once again put herself in a position of intimacy with him, strained but nonetheless very real.

"I don't know how you're sleeping so well. I can tell you that Steffan is probably not getting a wink of sleep."

Was she aware, he wondered, that she'd just given him a small portion of insight into Wythe? Since she'd been there she had given him zero information about Wythe—not that he'd needed her to tell him anything about the man. "It's easy for me to sleep. All my plans have been made. I'm ready."

"And you have complete faith in your plans?"

He nodded and watched a shadow chase across her face. He ached inside. He *wanted*. He lifted his hand and touched her cheek again, this time allowing his fingers to linger on the silken smoothness of her skin. But a mere touch didn't begin to satisfy him. Any other woman, any other time, any other circumstances, he would simply reach out and take. But she was not any other woman. "I'm sorry, Jillian." His voice was low and slightly gruff. "Because of something that's no fault of your own, you're going through hell."

She blinked. The last thing in the world she would have expected from him was an apology. "Are you sorry enough to call the whole thing off?"

His lips twisted. "You won't stop trying, will you?"

"Of course not. Why in the world would you think I'd accept for a minute what has happened to me?"

"I don't really, but I guess I hope."

"Hope?"

"Hope." For a long time she'd been only a name to him, someone who was a means to an end, someone he hadn't hesitated to use. But then he'd seen her, gotten to know her, and now heaven help him, he cared more than he should about whether or not she was happy. "And to answer your question, I'm sorry enough to do everything in my power to make you as comfortable as possible. But, Jillian, there's no calling it off, even if I wanted to."

"And you don't want to."

"No, I don't," he said flatly. "But I am sorry I had to involve you. I know the last thing in the world you want is for your stepfather to come after you and put himself in danger because of you. But for his sins he has to pay."

"Some people," she said quietly, "go a lifetime without paying for their sins."

"That's true enough, but for killing my family Wythe *will* pay."

His certainty made her so tense, she felt almost ill. "And if he does pay in the way you have planned, it will kill my mother. That's why I'm wondering—how many more innocent people must pay for Steffan's sin? Me? My mother? The people on this island?"

"I don't plan for anyone to pay but Wythe."

"That's not true. You planned all along to involve me, and *I've* had to pay."

"I don't see it as a great price. Just a slight disruption of your life for a very short period of time. Some people would view the situation as a vacation."

"You have no idea what you're talking about," she said, her voice shaking.

A muscle flexed in his jaw. Seeing his plan through her eyes was unexpectedly hard. But avenging the plane crash was so inbred in him, it literally would be beyond his ability to call it off. "I've apologized."

"And your apology makes it all right?"

"No," he said with quiet solemnity, his eyes never wavering from hers. "It doesn't.

And that's a sin *I* will have to live with my entire life."

She believed him, she thought. She absolutely believed what he said. Unfortunately it didn't make her feel one bit better, because she was still in the same precarious position.

"Were you exaggerating about what this is going to do to your mother?" he asked.

She sighed, then shook her head, irritated with both of them, but especially herself. He was her enemy. What was she doing even talking to him, much less sitting on his bed, feeling strangely at home, about to confide one of her worries to him? "I don't really know. It's hard to tell. She's already in bad health. There have been times I didn't see how she could live much longer, but she's always fooled me. But losing her husband could be the final blow. She worships him."

"After this is over, if you need help with her, all you have to do is let me know. Or if *you* need anything, anything at all . . ."

"I won't need your help."

His mouth tightened. "You mean you won't *accept* my help."

"That's what I mean." It appeared she had no choice but to let two powerful men play out a game of life and death, but once it was over, no matter what the outcome, she was going to reclaim her life, which meant getting

as far away as possible from both of those
men.

He watched her start to close up right before his eyes and hurried to try to stop it.
"What are you going to do when you leave
here? Go back to Maine? Be a waitress?"

"It's my life. It's what I do."

"Why? Your stepfather is one of the rich-
est men in the world."

"It's *his* money, not mine. Besides, I like
to work." It was true. But it was also true
she'd never wanted Steffan's money.

"And you actually enjoy living in a small
apartment?"

"I don't need a lot of space." She simply
needed to be able to leave that space if and
when she wanted. "Why are you asking about
my personal life?"

"Because it doesn't make sense to me."

"I've noticed that very little in this life
makes sense."

Realistically he knew that he couldn't,
shouldn't, expect anything of her, either now
or when this was all over. But it didn't stop
him from wanting. In fact his wanting was
getting out of control and he didn't know
what he was going to do about it. "I hear
you've been asking questions about me," he
said after a moment.

"What?" She didn't know what he was
talking about. Then she remembered and

rushed to clarify. "*I* didn't bring the subject up."

"Ah, don't tell me—Clay was trying to defend me."

"He thinks you're an honorable man."

He slowly grinned. She was opening back up, the shields she raised whenever she thought of what he had done to her were lowering. "But then I never kidnapped him, right?"

"There's certainly that." Her gaze stayed on his lips. He didn't need guards. His grin could disarm quite effectively. "Clay adores you."

His grin slowly faded. "I wonder what I'd have to do to get you to adore me."

"Adore you?" Their conversations had a way of taking unexpected turns that left her breathless. However, this particular turn was unequaled. Why would he ask something like that? There had to be some sort of ulterior motive behind the question.

"It's an impossible thought for you, isn't it?"

"Utterly preposterous."

"Really?"

"What are you doing?" In the stillness of the night, her voice was soft, tentative. She could barely hear anything but the beat of her heart. Something was happening between them, something strong and powerful, and she felt helpless to stop it.

"Are my sins against you really so unforgivable, Jillian?"

His eyes were glittering like dark emeralds and he had asked another strange question. But she had the answer to this one. "I've come to understand why you've done what you have, but I can't hate what you've done any less."

A hope that knew no reason sprang up in him. "Understanding is a first step."

"A first step to what?" Her tone was dubious.

"To many things."

The answer left a wide-open field of possibilities. And that field held danger. She ached to run her hands over his body, yet she'd never felt that way before, about any man. But his skin gleamed like dark satin in the lamplight, and beneath his skin she could see the subtle and intriguing shift of muscles. She eyed him warily. "Tell me something—why do you care what I feel about you?"

Her question stopped him in his mental tracks, making him think. She'd come to him for comfort, and he'd tried his best to give it. But she'd also come to him, smelling sweet, with nothing on but the fragile shift and eyes clear enough to see all the way to her soul. He supposed there were several ways he could answer her question—all more easily acceptable than the truth.

He wanted her.

In the end, he had no choice but to say exactly what he was thinking and feeling. "At the risk of frightening you," he explained slowly, huskily, "I find you very desirable. And I'd love nothing more right now than to pull you down on the bed and make love to you all night long."

Frightened wasn't exactly the word, she thought. Darkness frightened her. Being closed up in a place she couldn't get out of frightened her. But being desired by Sin Damaron merely alarmed her, bringing up myriad red flags. Because being desired by this man would be no easy or small thing. He would demand, he would take. He would also give.

And he would never force her into anything against her will. That knowledge *did* frighten her, because it left only one thing to be cautious of. *Herself.*

She'd never had a serious love and she had never wanted one. She'd become emotionally self-sufficient at an early age, and she'd never been a needy person. Several friendships in her adult life had developed into sexual relationships. But the passion had been casual, and each time she had moved on, each time without the need to look back.

Making love with Sin would be different. The certainty went bone deep in her. If they began an affair, the coming storm would be nothing compared with the effect he would have on the rest of her life.

"Jillian?"

She refocused on him. "Yes?"

"Don't worry," he said softly. "Nothing will happen unless it's what you want."

"Yes, I know."

His grin came back slowly and with an almost irresistible impact. "Well, then, as long as I'm being honest with you, I might as well tell you that I tried like hell not to want you."

Mr. Damaron is an honorable man. Clay's words came back to her, and once again she believed Sin. He was a man with honor who lived by his own rules. He had committed a sin to avenge a sin, and when Steffan came he would more than likely commit another one. He made her ache and for the first time in her life feel needy, in her eyes another sin. She didn't want to feel anything for him and she certainly didn't want to feel desire.

"But then here you are." His voice softened, roughened. "And to look at you is to want you."

A debilitating heat seeped into her bloodstream, flowing to every part of her body, and she found herself without words.

And he went on. "Before I met you I didn't care what happened to Wythe. Frankly I still don't, but for your sake . . ."

Her brow pleated as she tried to follow the new direction in which he had taken the conversation. "For my sake—what?"

"What if I tell you I will try my very best not to kill Wythe?"

"What are you doing, Sin? Trying to bargain with me?"

"Would bargaining work?"

"I suppose it would depend on *what* you were trying to bargain for."

"A point well taken."

"And the answer is?"

He reached out to her and traced the outline of her lips with the pad of his finger, making the blood flow fast inside her and grow hotter.

"No, Jillian, I'm not trying to bargain with you. Only gauge your reaction."

"I'm sorry, but I don't know how to react to that."

He dropped his hand, but his gaze lingered on her lips. "What if I say I'll do it anyway?" he asked, reluctantly lifting his gaze to her face. "That I'll try not to kill Wythe? That I'll try to turn him over to the authorities in one piece?"

"You'll try? You mean like you're trying to keep your hands off me?" She had no idea why she had said it.

"Do you want me to try harder?"

Yes, was the right answer, but she said something else instead. "You're getting off the subject."

"Me? Or you, Jillian? Which of us is getting off the subject? No matter what I'm talking about, the subject is still *you.*"

She swallowed. "Will you try not to kill Steffan?"

"Yes, I think I will try."

"Why?"

He spoke thoughtfully, but his eyes were glittering. "I don't think I want you to go through the rest of your life remembering me as the man who killed your stepfather."

She stared at him. Quite simply, Sin Damaron was the most devastating man she had ever known. He had kidnapped her, making her hate him, and then he had explained himself, making her understand his actions. Not only that, he had let her see the incredible gentleness and softness in him that he showed his daughter. And all the while he had showed concern for her.

He had told her he wanted her, but he had made no advances to her. He had touched her, he had burned her. He challenged her. And strangest of all, when she had needed to feel safe, she had run to him. And now, with every moment that passed, she was beginning to want him more and more. It was a trap, in and of itself, and panic began to rise in her once again. She glanced around, looking for a way out. "Would you mind changing that lightbulb for me now?"

"Now?"

"Yes, please."

He looked at her for several moments. "Should I ask why now?"

She wouldn't have an answer for him if he did. "No."

"Would it do any good at all to ask you to stay?"

She'd be tempted, and knowing that made her panic increase until she was nearly strangling with it. "No."

Without saying another word, he slid off the bed and moved across the room and out the door.

Her heart, she noticed, was beating as painfully and as hard as it had when she had first come looking for him. When she had awakened to the darkness, her first impulse, her only impulse, had been to run to him. She hadn't stopped to consider any other options.

In the next few days she *had* to be more careful, more cautious. No more visits in the night. No more conversations where she learned more about the man behind the powerful facade. No more opportunities for him to touch her, or for her to want to touch him. He had already turned her life upside down. She couldn't allow him to affect her life any more than he already had. She couldn't. . . .

Back in her room, Jillian tossed and turned, eventually falling into a troubled sleep. The next morning she awakened to find the bedside light burning brightly and the morning dawning over the island as beautiful and as peaceful as usual.

Lying in bed, she remembered the night, its darkness, the fear, and then the feelings of desire for Sin that had taken her unaware. There was nothing casual about that desire, nothing safe. Nothing at all right.

But just as she had learned how to deal with her fear, she would learn to deal with this new, burgeoning desire. Sin had made it clear it would be her decision whether or not they would make love, and her decision was *no*.

By Sin's own reckoning, Steffan would be coming soon, and then she would be free to go back to her life and Sin would go back to his. It was hard to believe that anything would ever be the same again, but it would be. It *had* to be. Dear Lord, she prayed, please let it be the same.

But minutes later the warm water from the shower stimulated her to further wakefulness and more memories of the night before. Jade eyes swam into her mind's vision, along with a magnetic smile that made her aware of wants and needs that she had never felt before.

But what she and Sin both were feeling couldn't be trusted, she told herself firmly. For different reasons, it was a time of great tension for both of them. Given her wants, she wouldn't have come to the island. Given Sin's wants, he would have ignored her during the time she was here. Anything they might be feeling was a product of an unnatural situation, more important, a temporary situation. It would all pass. It would . . .

After drying off, she selected underwear and a pair of jeans and a T-shirt to wear. Sin must have had an easy time packing for her, she thought wryly. He would have had very few decisions to make, since jeans and T-shirts were practically all she owned. She paused in her thoughts, trying to imagine Sin in her tiny apartment, touching not only her clothes but her panties and bras. He wouldn't have lingered. He would have wanted to get in and out as soon as possible. Besides, he might have touched her things, he might have touched her, but he hadn't touched her heart, nor did he know the secrets there.

Dressed, feeling edgy, she eyed the telephone. She knew she was expected to follow the routine, to place her order over the phone to Jacqueline and wait for it to be brought to her. But she earned her living waiting on other people. She wasn't accustomed to other people waiting on her, and it made her uncomfortable. Besides, she decided, she was simply too restless. She left the room in search of the kitchen.

Now that she'd been on the island a few days, she had a better idea of the layout of Sin's house. She was familiar with the wing her bedroom was in and, exploring, she discovered that the living areas of the house were open and airy, decked out in tropical colors. Very pleasant. Very livable. She'd probably never be in such a lovely place again, yet she couldn't even come close to enjoying it.

She made only one wrong turn before she found the kitchen.

Neither Clay nor Jacqueline was there. Instead she encountered two younger women, friendly, but quite bewildered to see her. Nevertheless they rushed to serve her and were dismayed when she waved them aside.

"It's all right," she said, giving them her best reassuring smile. "I'll help myself."

She poured herself a cup of coffee and wrapped a couple of freshly made breakfast rolls in a cloth napkin, then headed for the terrace outside her bedroom.

From her seat at the table there, she had a perfect view of paradise as it unfolded before her, with flowers, all colors of the rainbow, growing thick and plentiful, and their scents pervading the air. In the distance, sunlight danced on the blue-green water and glistened on the white sand.

Suddenly she frowned. Slowly setting down her coffee cup, she took a more careful look around her. Something was different. It seemed quieter than usual. And she couldn't spot any of the guards. The breeze still blew, but there was an unusual stillness. Even the birds in the trees seemed less active.

No, it had to be her imagination.

"Good morning."

She looked up, straight into a pair of familiar jade eyes, and her breath caught. His dark coloring stood out dramatically against the vivid blue, cloudless sky, and every cell in her body felt the impact of him, from his leanly muscled body, to his powerful sexuality, to his incredible good looks.

Before he had appeared, she'd thought she was fairly relaxed. She'd also thought she didn't want to see him. She'd been wrong on both counts. With Sin's appearance, the texture of the morning changed from quiet to thunderous, loud with unspoken feelings.

"I got a report from the kitchen. You upset the girls."

He was wearing a short-sleeve black polo shirt tucked into a pair of black trousers. He looked elegant, she thought, no matter what he wore.

She had planned to stay to herself today. She and Sin were able to have highly intimate conversations in the night. And when he touched her, her pulses raced and her skin burned, but the fact remained that she was not here for a holiday and she needed to remember that. "By waiting on myself?"

A slight grin played around his lips as he nodded. "That seems to be the gist of it."

"They shouldn't have been upset. I don't require much help to pour myself a cup of coffee and get a hot breakfast roll."

"No one does, but that's their job."

"I'm not used to people waiting on me, Sin. And surely the kitchen is not off-limits to everyone but the people who work there."

He dropped down into the chair opposite her, but didn't appear to relax. "If you ask me and most of the staff, the answer would be no. However"—he briefly grinned—"if you asked Jacqueline, the answer would be yes. I think it has to do with proprietorship."

She sighed. In the overall scheme of things, this was not a battle she needed to win. "Okay, Sin. I won't go back into the kitchen. After all, I'm not going to be here that much longer."

He studied her for a moment, his expression somber, then he glanced at his watch. "It's a beautiful day. Why don't you come outside?"

"I *am* outside."

"Yeah, sort of. But this terrace is sheltered by the house. I mean come down to the beach with me, or at least as far as the lower terrace."

Her pulse accelerated. This was the first time he had sought her company. "You want me to walk down to the beach with you?"

He nodded. "It's very nice down by the water."

She shouldn't be that surprised by the invitation. After all, last night he had told her he wanted her. But this morning there was nothing in his demeanor to suggest that his invitation stemmed from anything more than politeness. "Where's Lily? Doesn't she usually go down there every morning?"

"Reena is showing her how to make doll clothes."

"She must be very excited about that."

With another glance at his watch, he said, "I'm sure we'll get a fashion show later on this afternoon." He stood and held out his hand to her, and before she could stop herself she took it.

SEVEN

"Did you manage to get any sleep after you went back to your room last night?" he asked as he led her down the series of stone steps.

Somewhere along the way he had dropped her hand. And he was making chitchat. No reason why he shouldn't, Jillian reflected, except his demeanor definitely seemed different from usual. More awkward. Odd, since she felt sure he had known very few, if any, awkward moments in his life. He exuded self-confidence, and a middle-of-the-night visit from a woman, *any* woman, shouldn't be enough to throw him off stride. "Yes, I did. You?"

"Yes."

His profile was hard, his body controlled—normal. But he seemed to be avoiding looking at her. Did he regret the things he had said to her last night?

She shouldn't care one way or the other. Then again, she shouldn't have even come walking with him. "Is something wrong, Sin? I mean . . . is something bothering you?"

He threw a quick glance at her. "No. Why do you ask?"

She shrugged. "I don't know. You seem tense."

"Don't you think I have reason to be?"

"Last night you told me you weren't worried about Steffan. You said you were sleeping well." There was no reason to mention one particular subject he had brought up. She had no intention of sleeping with him, and therefore there was nothing for them to discuss. "Where are your guards this morning?"

"They're around."

A new tightness had entered his voice, she noted with curiosity. "Usually I can spot them."

"Really? Then maybe they're getting better at being unobtrusive."

"I would think that they'd be *more* of a deterrent if they *were* obtrusive."

"It depends on the effect one is going for."

"I suppose, but—" With a hand on her arm, he drew her to a stop beside him. They were on the last terrace, directly above the beach. And something *was* wrong. She wasn't sure what it was, but she knew she'd felt more at ease with him last night, sitting on his bed, than she did now.

"Sin, what—?"

"You're still worried about the guards? Why? *Who* exactly are you worried about?"

She stiffened at his curt tone. "If you're asking me whether I'm worried about you and the people on the island or whether I'm worried about Steffan, it's not a question that deserves an answer." It wasn't a question she could really answer either. She was worried about so much, and her worries were layers deep. She'd gotten to where she couldn't tell one worry from the other. They ran together and overlapped and all ended up in one giant pool of worries.

"You're right," he said after a moment. "It's not a question that deserves an answer."

She tried to push aside her unease about him. She had *real* problems, and she didn't need to fabricate any more. But she couldn't get past her preoccupation with him this morning. As beautiful as the surroundings were, she could concentrate on nothing but him.

Natural, she supposed. He was a dynamic, vital man with a masculinity that could be as treacherous as a riptide. He was standing with his legs apart, his hands in his slacks pocket, the wind blowing his dark hair as he scanned the horizon. He looked very contained, very hard, superimposed against the wild beauty of the island.

"Sin?"

"Yes?" His tone was absent.

She wanted him to give her some indication of what was wrong, but she couldn't think of what to say. "Do you live here year-round?" It was a stupid, inane question, but she couldn't think of a better one.

"No. My main home is in New York, but I come here as often as possible. So do my cousins. It's really nice when we can all be here together."

"It must be nice to be a member of a close family." Almost immediately she realized it had been the wrong thing to say. And sure enough, he picked up on it.

For the first time that morning he really looked at her. "You're obviously close to your family, your mother and stepfather. You seem to go home often."

She shook her head. "The Middle East is not my home. I go there to see my mother, that's all. My home is in America."

"In Maine?"

"Wherever I happen to be."

He nodded, his gaze on her hair as the wind ruffled through it. "I understand you move a lot."

She sighed, sorry now that she had even

come with him. "I suppose you were told that by someone you had investigating me."

"You suppose right."

"That's really charming, Sin."

His brows raised. "It was necessary."

"Depends on whose point of view."

"Naturally I was speaking from my point of view."

"Naturally." She'd done her best to live a quiet, unobtrusive life, yet she'd still attracted attention. Sin had found her, kidnapped her, and on a certain level, seduced her.

The latter was hard for her to believe, but it was true.

Because if he hadn't seduced her, why else would she be with him this morning? Why else would she be trying so hard to find a topic of conversation that he would talk to her about? And why else would *she* be the one who was now feeling awkward?

She didn't understand why Sin had sought her out and asked her to come for a walk with him. He didn't seem to be interested in her or in talking to her. And she was just about ready to go back to her room. "Sin, was there some particular reason you wanted to see me this morning?"

She heard a sound but didn't immediately register what it was.

He turned to her, a strange expression on his face. "Jillian . . ."

"What—?" She looked toward the sound and saw an airplane flying low over the ocean, coming straight for the island. "Is that one of yours?" Even as she asked she knew it wasn't. As the plane drew closer and she saw its markings, she turned to him, stricken. "Steffan? Is that *Steffan*?"

"It's his plane," he said tightly, "but he's probably not on board. He's smarter than that. He wouldn't come at us in plain sight, in the daylight, straight over the middle of the island. It's a reconnaissance mission."

"A recon—?" She stopped as cold realization washed over her. "You knew," she whispered in shock. "You knew that plane was coming."

He lifted his head as the plane flew over them, his gaze following its progress. "We picked it up on radar while it was still miles away."

"And you brought me out here so that whoever's on that plane could see me?" Even in the face of his admission, she was having a hard time believing that he had really done this to her. She felt stupid, slow, and incredibly hurt.

He looked back at her, his green eyes dark with emotion she couldn't decipher. "That's right."

Over his shoulder she saw Lion and several other men emerging from the house.

"And you had all the guards stay out of sight so Steffan wouldn't be able to tell what and where your defenses are."

He nodded. "There's no telling what sort of equipment they had on that plane. Photographic for sure. Perhaps thermal imaging. But they still won't be able to count the people in the houses."

"But they will go back to Steffan with pictures confirming I'm here." She was crushed by his deception, and at the same time, fury rose steadily in her, threatening to choke her. "Tell me something. Why the trickery with me? Why pretend you wanted to spend time with me? Why not just drag me down here?"

"Jillian, I'm sorry—"

"*Why?*" Tears of anger and hurt stung her eyes; furiously she blinked them back. "I'm your captive, right? That means *you* have the power. I have to do what you say. Hell, you could have chloroformed me again. Why not? Then you could have simply laid me down in one of the chaise longues. It would have looked like I was sunning myself. I'm sure Steffan would have gotten a big kick out of that."

"I had no intention of using chloroform on you again. It was bad enough I had to do it once."

She gave a harsh laugh. "Scruples, Sin? Don't you think it's a little late for them?"

His mouth tightened grimly. "I had no choice. You wouldn't have come if I'd told you the truth."

"You're very right. I wouldn't have." She turned, moving away from him, and stumbled in her haste.

With lightning swiftness he reached out and grasped her arm. "Jillian, don't—"

"Just leave me alone, Sin." She jerked away from him and took off running, down the final steps that led to the beach and onto the sand. Once there, she kept running.

"Jillian." He started after her, but then stopped. He couldn't think of one thing he could say to her. She was in pain, pain he had caused, and there was no way he could make the pain go away.

"Do you want me to send someone after her?" Lion asked, coming up behind him.

"No. Let her be." His hands balled into fists as his gaze followed her. *"Dammit.* On second thought, have someone keep an eye on her to make sure she doesn't hurt herself."

"Consider it done." Lion headed back toward the house in a trot.

Sin stayed where he was, staring after her. The pain in her eyes as she'd realized what he'd done had cut him to the bone. But there had been no other way to accomplish what had to be done. Having her on the terrace to be photographed was the surest and fastest way to give Wythe conclusive proof that his stepdaughter had been abducted. Now there would be no delay. Once Wythe had a look at the recon photos, he'd formulate a plan and put it into action immediately. Exactly as Sin wanted.

He cursed aloud. If only there'd been some way not to hurt Jillian.

Jillian had no idea where she was going.

She ran along the water's edge, hardly noticing when the beach began to curve gently, following the island's natural contour. All she cared about was getting away from Sin, as far and as fast as she could. It didn't matter that he had been kind to her, concerned about her. It didn't matter that every time she saw him, her attraction for him grew. He had lied to her.

She ran over driftwood and around rocks. She ran until she developed a stitch in her side, until she ran out of breath, until she couldn't go one step farther.

Panting, struggling for air, she finally collapsed onto the sand.

Sin paced the length of the upper terrace, a walkie-talkie in his hand, impatiently waiting for a report, his gaze constantly scanning the area for any sign of Jillian. As time passed he grew more and more anxious. Finally the walkie-talkie crackled to life in his hand.

"She's stopped at Turquoise Cove, Sin."

"What's she doing?"

"Nothing. Just sitting there. I think she's probably trying to catch her breath. That was quite a run she went on."

"Is she okay?"

"She didn't fall once, if that's what you mean. She's not hurt."

He didn't know what the hell he meant. "Stay with her." He clicked off and sent a bleak look at Lion.

"Don't beat yourself up," his cousin said softly. "She's okay."

"If there'd only been another way."

"But there wasn't and you know it."

He knew it, but the knowledge didn't stop him from second-guessing himself. With everything that was in him, he believed his cause was just. But where Jillian was concerned, he couldn't stop from feeling lower than low.

Jillian looked around and realized she didn't have a clue where she was. Turquoise waters, whiter than white sand, vibrantly colored flowers—the area looked exactly like the part of the island in front of Sin's house.

Not that it mattered. How lost could she be on an island? Besides, she was sure someone would come get her. She was too valuable. The thought stiffened her backbone.

No. She had no intention of being led back to Sin's house like some recalcitrant child. Or worse, like the prisoner she was.

Damn! It was *stupid* of her to let Sin hurt her like this.

She should know that leopards *never* changed their spots.

She should have remembered that scorpions were incapable of doing *anything* but stinging.

And she should have definitely learned by now that a sinner committed one sin right after the other.

Sin was using her, had been using her from the first. She wouldn't forget it again.

It was a long time before the walkie-talkie once more crackled in Sin's hand. "Yes?"

"She's started back toward the house—walking."

"Stay with her. Let me know if she takes a detour." He shot Lion a look of despair. "She doesn't deserve this, *any* of this."

"Try to remember, Sin—her hurt is only mental, not physical."

Not like our parents. Lion didn't say it, but

the words were there between them. Sin nodded in understanding. "I'll be so glad when
this is all over, for more than one reason.
Damm it, I should have never let her take off
like that."

Over an hour passed, then the walkie-
talkie crackled again. "Yes?"

"She's entering the house by the side
door."

"Thanks." He immediately turned for the
house, but then stopped. She needed time
alone, he told himself. There would be no
point in going to her. She would be too angry
to listen to him. And besides, what could he
really say to her that he hadn't already said?
No, he had to stay away from her, at least for
the rest of the day. Give her time . . .

Jillian couldn't stop trembling. Sweat covered her body, making her T-shirt stick to her
skin. She wasn't used to running, not even to
exercise, and even though she'd walked on her
return trip, her body was paying for her im-
pulsive action. Her muscles were tightening,
complaining. Plus, her emotions were still all
over the place—high, low, left, right, anger,
hurt, confusion.

She stripped out of her clothes, climbed
into the marble shower, and turned the water
to as hot as she could stand it. The water

stung her skin, its heat soothed her muscles, the steam swirled around her, but still she couldn't relax. She shut her eyes and willed the water to do its work. Unfortunately her mind wandered straight to Sin.

He had made her comfortable here on the island, *so* comfortable that when she looked into his eyes and felt his hands on her skin, she tended to forget that all she was to him was bait. He could want her—in fact, she believed him when he said he did—and at the same time he could, without a second thought, use her to lure Steffan into his trap.

Compartmentalizing was foreign to her. Apparently so was using common sense when she was with Sin. She forgot to protect herself. Truthfully, when she was with Sin, she forgot everything but him.

Steffan would be furious when he saw the photographs of her, standing with Sin, which, of course, was exactly what Sin wanted. If Steffan was angry he might make mistakes. . . .

The water rained down on her, as did feelings of helplessness and confusion. What in the world was she going to do now?

The enormity of her dilemma weighed heavily on her, sapping the last of her strength so that even standing became a struggle. That she hadn't eaten this morning didn't help. Neither did thoroughly exhausting herself during her desperate flight from Sin.

She began to feel light-headed and had to lean against the marble wall for support. For her to faint now, to lose that basic hold on self-control, would be the ultimate humiliation. And she refused to inflict that on herself.

After taking a couple of fortifying breaths, she leaned forward to reach for the brass faucet and turn off the water. Big mistake, she realized instantly. The light-headedness returned with a vengeance. She swayed, her knees buckled, and her head struck the faucet.

Pain.

Darkness.

"Lord, Jillian, are you all right?"

"What—?" Her head was hurting, she realized with puzzlement.

"Jillian? Open your eyes and look at me."

Opening her eyes seemed to require more energy than she had, but the urgency of Sin's voice pulled at her, commanding her to obey him.

"Jillian?"

In the end, his will was stronger than hers, and slowly her lids lifted, and she looked up into Sin's ashen face. "W-what are you doing here?"

"I came to check on you, and when there

was no answer at your door I walked in. Thank God I did. I was just in time to hear you cry out." He tentatively touched her forehead. "What in the hell happened?" The gentleness of his touch was in sharp contrast to the harshness of his voice.

"I—I just fell. It's nothing."

"God, Jillian, you stop my heart. You really do,"

What had he said? He sounded so upset. She reached up to touch her temple and her fingers came away sticky with blood. She was lying on the bathroom floor, she realized. Water misted outward from the shower, drenching her and the floor. Good Lord, she was naked. "I—I've got to get dressed." Simultaneously she tried to get up and cover herself with her hands, but her efforts were futile and Sin was faster.

With a muffled oath, he turned off the shower, then scooped her into his arms and carried her into the bedroom. There, still cursing to himself, he carefully laid her on the bed.

"If I hadn't come when I did—"

She was barely listening to him. Her head was now throbbing, focusing her attention inward toward the pain. And she was still naked. "Sin—"

Instinctively she tugged at the comforter, attempting to pull it over her, but he was already leaning over her to the opposite side of the bed and pulling the comforter up and sideways until it covered her.

"Is that better?"

She nodded, then grimaced at the pain.

"Dammit, Jillian. You're really hurt. What in the hell happened?" he repeated.

He spoke quietly, but his anxiety came through loud and clear, practically hammering at her. She closed her eyes against its force. "It's nothing. I just need to lie here for a minute."

"Right," he muttered gruffly. "Stay here. Be still. I'll be right back."

He couldn't stop shaking as he hurried into the bathroom. When he thought of that awful moment when he had first caught sight of her, lying crumpled at the bottom of the shower, blood flowing freely down the side of her face, his stomach roiled. If the blow to her head had been a little harder, she might have killed herself. As it was, it was a very serious injury. She might need tests, hospitalization.

Rapidly sorting through options, he moistened a washcloth and returned to sit on the bed beside her.

His weight on the mattress jarred her slightly, drawing a moan from her.

"God, I'm sorry, Jillian."

"I fell," she mumbled. "You didn't push me."

In the mood he was in right now, he thought grimly, he could debate the blame. He pressed the washcloth over the cut on her forehead. She flinched, even though he was being extremely gentle. "I'm afraid you might have a concussion."

"No. It's not that serious. Just a minor—"

"You were unconscious when I got to you, Jillian. That's not minor. This cut . . . there was so much blood, but"—he studied the cut and began cleaning it—"I don't think you're going to need stitches. That's amazing. It's not that big. . . ."

He was basically talking to himself, and she kept her eyes closed. Right now, with her head hurting, he was simply too much for her to deal with. Anger and frustration vibrated off him in strong waves, bombarding her body almost as much as the throbbing pain was. And yes, she could also feel his concern. And no matter how much she wished differently, his concern affected her more than his anger.

"I think a butterfly bandage is going to fix this cut." Relief filled his tone. "Stay put."

The mattress moved again as he got up. She had no more than a minute or two to herself before he was back, pressing a bandage to the cut.

"Good," she murmured when he was finished. "That will fix it. Thank you."

"It will fix the cut, but you could still have a concussion."

"No, that's not possible. It's not that serious. I know it's not. I couldn't have been out more than a few seconds."

"I realize that, but you've got a lump that's already coming up, and whether you like it or not, I'm going to keep an eye on you."

At that, she opened her eyes and was surprised at how pale he looked. "I *don't* like it." She tried to push herself up, but a new light-headedness defeated her. Her head fell back onto the pillow.

"See?"

"No, I don't see." She hated feeling helpless and she hated that Sin looked so genuinely anxious about her. She would have cried except for a very firm determination not to cry in front of him. "I'll be fine in just a few minutes."

"I hope so, but I'm still going to keep an eye on you. Head injuries might seem minor at first, but they can have major aftereffects."

She stifled a groan. "Just leave me alone."

"Sorry, but I can't." His voice was calm, firm. "If it will make you feel any better, you can look at this as if I'm not giving you a choice, because you'd be right. But you can also look at this as if I'm very worried about you and you'd also be right. Either way, I plan to stay close."

She couldn't come up with a thing to say to that. She had enough wits about her to realize that she wasn't up to fighting him. He was so close, his strength focused totally on her. For now, anyway, it was easier to give in to him. "Would you at least leave so that I can put some clothes on?"

He hesitated, then reached out for the phone. "I'll call Jacqueline to come in and help you."

Her hand landed on top of his, stalling his effort to dial. "You will do no such thing."

"But what if you fall again?"

"I won't."

His mouth tightened. "Why are you being so stubborn about this? You're hurt. You need help."

"No, I don't. And I'm not being stubborn. I'm simply trying to deal with this the best way I can."

Momentarily defeated by her strong will, he slowly exhaled. "All right, but I'll be right outside the door. If you get dizzy or need anything, call me." He stood and looked down at her with a dark, gleaming gaze. "You've got five minutes before I come back in."

"Give me ten."

"Six."

The heated look in his eyes was almost as debilitating as the fall had been. But with some effort, she was able to infuse a modicum of sarcasm into her tone. "You're too good to me."

His expression darkened even more. "I'm sorry, Jillian."

Another apology, another pain. She shut her eyes, but not even that could block him out. There was such power in him, such intensity, that even after he left the room, she could still feel his presence.

Very carefully she threw back the comforter and slid to her feet. But the light-headedness forced her to fling out a steadying hand to the bedside table. After a few moments she cautiously proceeded to the closet.

Even if it hadn't been late afternoon, she would have still bypassed her jeans and T-shirts for the smoke-blue gauze caftan she found in the closet, the *softest* garment there. She had no idea whose it was, and she didn't care. It wouldn't be hanging in a guest room if it wasn't meant to be used. After putting it on, she headed for the bathroom, where she found an aspirin bottle in the medicine cabinet. She took two, then returned to bed, which is where Sin found her a few minutes later.

"Were you watching a clock the whole time?" she murmured.

"I checked on Lily," he said, ignoring her sarcasm. He held out a glass of water and two capsules. "Take these."

"I've already taken aspirin. Don't you have something you should be doing, like setting traps?"

"I'm doing what I need to be doing." He drew a chair close to the bed and sat down. "Are you hungry?"

"No." She didn't want him to stay with her. She was too disturbed, still too upset. And his presence only stirred up her emotions more.

"Has the aspirin started to work yet?"

She closed her eyes. "No."

"Are you going to talk to me?"

"No."

He sighed and rubbed his eyes, surprised to find pain there. He downed the two capsules himself. "I've already told you I'm sorry. What else can I do?"

"You can stop telling me you're sorry. You can leave me alone. You can make sure I don't see you again until all this is over." Even to her ears, she sounded petulant, but it was either that or tears.

"I can't do that, Jillian."

His voice was as soft as velvet, reaching out to stroke her. She turned her face into the pillow. He'd coolly tricked her for his own purposes, and now with gentleness and tenderness he was trying to take care of her. Another trick, she was sure. Just as she was sure that she couldn't let him take care of her. He was too dangerous. She'd already admitted to herself that he made her forget. And now she was going to have to admit something else. She was beginning to care about him.

EIGHT

The night seemed longer than forever. At times the clock barely moved. Sin knew *he* didn't move, not from the chair beside the bed. Watching Jillian sleep was mesmerizing.

"This is really ridiculous," she said grouchily when she awoke briefly at one point to find him still sitting there.

He smiled. "I agree." It *was* ridiculous for him to remain in the room. It was also torturous, watching her. She lay on her back, her head turned to the pillow, her thick lashes bunched against her cheeks. One arm was raised, her palm out, her fingers curled downward. The small area above her temple was slightly swollen and purple. She looked very fragile, very vulnerable, very desirable.

Several hours ago he'd quit worrying about whether or not she had a concussion.

But he'd kept sitting there. He'd had no real choice. No matter how hard he tried, he couldn't tear himself away from her bedside. She was doing nothing, yet she still enticed him.

She'd insisted that the bedside light stay on, but she wouldn't say why. He liked it on because it allowed him to see her, but he couldn't help wondering what was behind her need to have it on. He'd bet money it was more than a simple fear of the dark. Too much about the way she lived didn't make sense to him.

To complicate an already complicated situation, he was discovering that she was as complex as she was beautiful. And tempting.

As she breathed, her breasts rose and fell above the low lace edge of the caftan, and he could see the faint shadow of her nipple through the thin blue gauze material. And he remembered. . . .

He remembered that terrible moment when he found her on the shower floor, blood streaming from the cut. He'd been terrified for her. Amazing, really—such strong emotion for someone who wasn't supposed to make a ripple in his life.

Good Lord in heaven—she'd made a tidal wave.

There was also another moment he couldn't forget, a moment when a flare of need had pierced his fear. It had happened when he had laid her down on the bed and he'd seen her naked body, gleaming with moisture, her skin pale and silky, her breasts high and round, her nipples rose-colored and tight.

That moment had passed as his fear had quickly rushed back, but now that he knew she was going to be all right, he couldn't keep the image from his mind.

She stirred, moaning in her sleep.

Jillian knew she was dreaming. It was the same dream she'd had since she was a little girl. And each time the dream came she was afraid all over again.

There was the darkness, always the darkness. It was all around her, suffocating her, threatening.

There was the huge shape, looming above her . . . and there were the awful, ugly words that kept coming at her. . . .

And the strangling fear she couldn't control.

And the scissors . . .

She reached for them, felt her hand close around them.

"Jillian? Jillian?"

Hands gripped her arms. She lashed out, fighting against the restraint with all her might.

"Jillian, honey, be still. I'm not going to hurt you."

"*No!*" she yelled in the dream. In reality. *The scissors . . . The scissors . . .*

"Wake up, Jillian. Wake up, sweetheart."

It was Sin's voice, calling to her through the darkness. And he had called her sweetheart. . . .

She woke abruptly and saw him leaning over her, his dark green eyes glittering down at her with concern. Such a familiar sight.

Without a thought, without a word, she sat up and reached for him, pulling him down to sit beside her on the bed, threading her arms around his neck. She hung on to him as if he were a life raft and she was going down for the third time in a turbulent sea. He exuded strength and warmth, two things she desperately needed right now.

"What's wrong?" His voice was husky. "Tell me." He ran his hand over her hair, stroking her, soothing her.

"I don't know." His shirt felt smooth beneath her cheek and carried his musky scent. "I can't."

Careful not to touch the swollen bruise on her forehead, he lightly ran his fingers through her hair. "You sounded like you were fighting your way through a dream."

As much as she wanted to stay exactly where she was, safe in his arms, she knew she shouldn't, couldn't. Safety and Sin were two words that didn't belong together, even if right now it felt as if they did. But it was a temporary illusion born out of her own need. With a sigh she pushed away from him. "Yes, I guess I was."

"What were you dreaming about?"

"I—I really can't remember." If only that were the truth. Unfortunately she knew the dream well. Even awake, she never really got away from it.

He was there in the darkness, watching, waiting, ready to hurt her.

The scissors, the points long and sharp, were lying there beside her. She didn't want to use them, but . . . Her tears filled her eyes, almost blinding her. She reached out. . . .

"You don't remember?"

Her tongue flicked out to lick her dry lips. She'd never been able to talk about the dream, not to anyone. It was too awful, too *real.* "Not really. I'm fine now."

The scissors—they were covered with blood.

"Jillian?"

His voice was so gentle, just as it had been when she had heard it calling her out of the dream. Once again, she realized, she had reached out to him when she had been frightened. She'd done it without thinking, and even more amazing, she'd done it without stopping to stew about the fact that he was using her. And he hadn't let her down. He'd been there to bring her out of the darkness. He was with her now, soothing her out of the dream.

Suddenly she realized that in her own way, *she* was using him—his strength, his kindness, his concern for her. If it weren't for him, she would still be caught in the dream. If it weren't for him, she would still be frightened out of her mind.

Shock rocked through her at the knowledge. Reaching out to someone to calm her fears was completely new to her. She'd been alone for so long. She'd *wanted* to be alone. But now . . .

He lightly drew a finger along her jawline, regaining her attention. "How's your head?"

"It's better." Truthfully, the dream and his nearness had eclipsed the throb in her head. But now that she thought about it, she realized she was still feeling a dull ache. "Actually, I think I'll take a couple of aspirin."

"I'll get them for you."

"No." She reached out and put a hand on his arm. "I need to get up."

He looked down at her hand, then back at her. "Okay, but let me help you." He stood and gently pulled her to her feet. "Do you need me to go with you?"

"No." Having someone hovering over her was also new to her. She didn't know whether to feel protected or smothered, reassured or annoyed.

"I'll wait here until you get back."

She wasn't annoyed and she didn't argue. The truth was, she wanted him there. And a wry thought came out of nowhere to surprise her. It seemed that for one reason or another, she was fated to spend part of every night with him.

In the bathroom, a glance in the mirror startled her. A purple swelling marked the left side of her forehead. Wonderful, just wonderful. She pressed a warm cloth to her face for several moments, then finger-combed her hair to partially cover the bruise. After downing the aspirin, she went back into the bedroom.

Sin was waiting for her, as she knew he would be. She could depend on him, she thought, because she now understood his contradictions. He was a man who was safe and solid, yet someone who without compunction could hold her against her will. He was a man who had the ability to lessen the horror of a nightmare with his presence, but he would stop at nothing to gain his revenge. And he was also the man who made her blood heat, with anger, with desire.

Lord help her, she wanted him.

Even as she thought it she called herself crazy.

Slowly she walked across the shadowed

room until she was on the opposite side of the bed from him. She should have felt easier, with the bed between them, but she didn't. There seemed to be a denseness in the air, as if it were filled with a multitude of unspoken words. And those words disturbed her. Because the words were of feelings, and once spoken, they could be exceedingly dangerous. "I'm going to be fine now, Sin."

He nodded, his expression unreadable. "That's good."

Tension floated between them and around them, touching her, putting pressure on her. She had a decision to make. She knew what it should be, but it was harder than she expected. Much harder. Needing support, she rested one knee on the bed. "You're probably tired."

"I'm fine."

"There's no reason for you to stay here any longer. You should go to your room and get some sleep."

"Is that what you want?"

His voice rasped across her nerves.

"Yes, it is."

He nodded, but didn't move. His gaze was fixed on her. "Jillian . . . I've already apologized to you for everything."

She gestured, trying to stop him before he went any further. She didn't want to hear another apology from him. He sounded too sincere, so sincere she at times was tempted to forgive him. "An apology means nothing if you have no intention of correcting or changing what you've done wrong."

"You're probably right, but I needed to apologize to you."

"And you have. Now please leave."

"In a minute. There's something else I want to say."

She rubbed her bare arms. "You've already said too much." And she'd listened too much, because she had, she was *feeling* way too much.

Restlessly he rubbed the back of his neck and started to pace. "Jillian, I'm used to arranging the world to my liking."

She hugged herself, trying to keep her feelings in. "You don't have to tell me that. I'm here against my will because of that particular penchant of yours. Need a pawn? A hostage? No problem. Just snatch Jillian off a beach. Piece of cake."

He stopped and skewered her with a look. "That's right—I captured you. And then, Jillian, you captured me."

She outwardly stilled, but inside, heat curled. "I don't know what you're talking about." Her mind didn't *want* to know, but she was very much afraid her heart already knew. "I've done nothing."

He half smiled. "Done nothing except

make me want you. I've got a lot of power, Jillian, but against you I have none."

"You hold *all* the power, Sin."

He started toward her, his expression as intense and as serious as she'd ever seen it. She had to fight not to back away from him, but she did straighten, putting both feet on the floor.

"I hold the power because I'm keeping you here against your will. You're right about that, but that's where my power ends."

He stopped within arm's reach of her, and her heart thumped hard against her rib cage. He was beginning to make sense to her.

"If we were in any other circumstances," he whispered roughly, "I would pursue you with everything I have. I'd go to the end of the earth for you if I had to. I wouldn't stop at anything. I wouldn't rest until I had you." His eyes burned dark and bright with a fire she had never seen before. "But I've put you through enough. I can't allow myself to coerce you in any other way, shape, or form. It wouldn't be right. But it also doesn't change how I feel about you. I want to make love to you until neither one of us can think about anything but how we feel and how we make each other feel."

She was stunned into silence. She hadn't been prepared for his words, just as she wasn't prepared when he leaned down and pressed his lips to hers. At the first touch, an electric thrill jolted her and he seemed to hesitate. Then with a gruff murmur, he brought his mouth down on hers in a full, deep kiss that singed her through and through, leaving no part of her untouched or unaffected. So much so that when he broke off the kiss, it left her bereft.

"Good night."

And then she was alone.

She raised her hand and touched her lips where the heat still lingered. And she realized she was shaking.

She wanted him. The truth was stark, simple, astounding.

She could taste her desire for him. She could *feel* it, starting inside her body and working outward to her skin. If she looked in the mirror, she was positive she'd be able to see that desire on her face, her skin, glowing, pulsing.

And all he'd done was kiss her. Take care of her. Be concerned about her. Touch her . . .

If she were being objective, she supposed this desire she felt for him wasn't so unusual. She had been thrown in close quarters with a handsome, compelling man in a situation that was inherently tense. It was only natural that from the first, feelings had run high between them and that heat of all kinds had ignited.

The heat of anger, the heat of frustration, the heat of the effort of trying to keep a natural and effortless passion submerged.

And she couldn't get away from the fact that after he'd brought her to the island, it had been *she* who had done the throwing, the advancing, the putting herself in his path whenever possible.

But tonight he'd walked away from her. His honor wouldn't let him pursue her.

She looked around the bedroom. It seemed an exceptionally still night, with the only sound that of her own breathing. She had never minded being alone. In fact, she usually enjoyed being alone. But tonight, with Sin just down the hall from her, she found she didn't want to be in this big room without him. She didn't want to go the rest of the night without seeing him again, without his touch, his kiss. She didn't want to go the rest of the night without *him*.

Sin lay back against a pile of pillows, showered but not yet dressed for bed, his eyes closed against the bedside light that he hadn't gotten around to turning off yet. The battle he'd fought with himself had left him exhausted. Turning his back on Jillian and walking out of her room had been the hardest thing he'd ever had to do.

He prided himself on being a person of control. But one look at Jillian could make him go hard, make him sweat, make him ache. And she didn't have the faintest idea.

True, he'd confessed to her that he wanted her, but he'd tried his best to hide the extent of his need for her. She had more than enough to deal with at present. He'd barged into her life, torn it apart, and he wasn't through yet. He needed to leave her completely alone.

But God help him, he didn't know if he could. . . .

He heard the door open and close, then he saw her standing just inside the room, appearing like a magical manifestation of his desire. "Jillian?"

She hesitated a moment, then shrugged. "I couldn't stay away."

Right from the first, from the first few hours he had spent in Maine observing her, he'd wanted her. And now he was going to have her.

With a rough sound of relief he held out his arms and she ran to him, climbing onto the bed and going into his arms.

He wouldn't question why she was here, he told himself, crushing his mouth down on hers and letting himself go completely. For this short time, deep in the night, she would be his. And that was all he could ask.

He increased the pressure of his mouth against hers, kissing her deeply and hard, unable to get enough of her taste. Tremors racked his body. He'd held his desire in for so long that now that she was in his arms he couldn't hold himself back.

"Wait," she whispered, and pulled away. Involuntarily his hands clenched, loath to let her go. "Wait," she said again, and with a soft smile, she rose up on her knees and pulled her caftan up and over her head. She flung it away then came down to him again. Shock jolted through him at the feel of her naked skin against his, then a river of fire coursed through him, and he had to fight to slow himself down.

Tremors of need shivered over her skin. She'd made her decision and there was no thought of going back. By his own account they weren't going to have much time together. Perhaps that was why she clung to him so hard, kissed him so frantically. This night would pass and then she'd be alone again. But for now she was going to take and then take some more. As the years passed, she'd have many regrets, but she would never regret this night.

She smoothed her hands over his bare chest, then his shoulders and back, savoring the feel of his muscles shifting and rolling beneath the sleek, satinlike texture of his skin.

She'd never known anything like the hunger she felt for him. She was *consumed* by it, by him. They'd known each other such a short time, yet it seemed she'd waited forever to have him inside her, and she found she couldn't wait another moment.

She clutched at him and pressed her face against the strong column of his neck. "Sin. Make love to me. Now."

His control almost shredded, he didn't need the encouragement. He moved over her and arranged himself between her legs. Then he pulled back his hips and thrust into her, and as he did he felt her open for him and take him deep into her tight velvet depths. Heaven shuddered through him, followed by thunderous pleasure.

And it didn't stop.

She was silk enchantment, utter bliss. He'd never tasted anything sweeter than her skin, never felt anything softer. The night lay before them, but he was hit by the sure feeling that there wasn't enough time for him to make love to her the way he wanted. There'd *never* be enough time.

Darkness clustered all around them. She lay with him in a golden pool of light, her body straining against his, their limbs entwined. She was caught up in a savage, heated rhythm with him that was exclusively their own. Beyond them was the rush and roar of the ocean. Inside, there was a turbulence and a torment of basic, primitive need.

With each of his touches, with each of his kisses, she could feel herself coming more and more alive. Her skin soaked up his touch as if it were a desert thirsting for rain.

It was heaven, being in his arms, being filled up with him; it was hell. And she had no one to blame but herself. She knew exactly what she was doing. For better or worse she was exactly where she wanted to be.

Her body craved his. With murmured words and urgent motions she urged him deeper into her, harder. Fire streaked through her, stayed, gathered, grew, tightened. She bucked beneath him, wanting, reaching, climbing. And then suddenly her climax gripped her, taking control of her body, ripping through her, and then hurling her over the burning edge of ecstasy.

And then she reached for him again.

NINE

With a gasp, Jillian awoke all at once. She was in Sin's bedroom, naked, with the softness of his sheets tangled around her legs and the dark sensual scent of him all around her. But when she opened her eyes, she was alone.

She shut her eyes again.

The last thing she remembered was falling asleep in Sin's arms. After hours of lovemaking, it had seemed a very natural thing to do, to allow herself to relax against him and fall asleep with her legs entwined with his.

She silently groaned. Last night had been truly extraordinary. For the first time she had learned what true passion was all about. For the first time she'd experienced a climax. And that had been only the first of the revelations that had unfolded during the night. She had amazed herself at her capacity for passion with Sin.

The fire had been constant, the pleasure unimaginable. She'd known, even then, that by coming to his room, she was making an impossible situation worse. But at that moment it hadn't mattered to her what he'd done or what he was about to do. It had seemed right to go to him, and so she had.

A sin? No. A mistake? It couldn't be anything else. But she had made the mistake knowingly and willingly and in return had learned how deep pleasure could be with Sin and how high her body and spirit could soar.

But now it was day, Sin was gone, and she had to face the consequences of her actions. Alone, once again.

She slipped from his bed and made her way back to her room. In the bathroom she assessed her image in the mirror. She looked the same as she had yesterday, except for the bruise and the small butterfly bandage on her forehead. Idly she swept a few strands of her hair down to cover the bruise, then looked at herself again. Was it her imagination or did her lips look slightly swollen? She lightly touched her bottom lip. No, it wasn't her imagination. Her lips *were* swollen. And her skin was sensitive, glowing.

Fleetingly her mind went to the woman who had been Lily's mother. Had she felt this way after a night of lovemaking with Sin? Special? As if surely he had never made love to any other woman as he had with her? So thoroughly. So passionately. Was that why she had fallen so hard for him? Hard enough that she hadn't wanted to go on living without him?

Jillian frowned. It was a stupid thought. She wasn't that woman. She might have fallen for Sin to the point that she wanted him, but she didn't love him. How could she? And she certainly wouldn't be destroyed when they parted.

She sighed heavily. *Enough*, she told herself. Enough thinking about Sin and what would or wouldn't be. She didn't know what the hours ahead would bring, but she did know that she'd better be prepared for anything.

She showered and dressed and then found herself at a loss as to what she should do next. Standing in the middle of her room, she realized that she'd actually hoped that Sin would come find her.

Why hadn't he been there beside her when she'd woken up? she wondered once more.

"Dammit, Jillian," she muttered softly. "Quit being so foolish."

With a singleness of purpose she was far from feeling, she walked out onto her terrace to be greeted by yet another perfect day. The vivid, tropical landscape had become very familiar to her, she reflected, and she wouldn't forget it once she left. In fact, she didn't think she would forget even one minute she had spent on the island, and she knew for a fact she wouldn't forget the people. Sin . . . the man with the dark green eyes and the gentle hands that could ignite fire and the hard body that could take her to peak after peak and still make her want more.

Foolish, she reminded herself.

Below her, Lion sat on the main terrace, talking to a man she didn't think she'd seen before. The silver streak in his hair, however, gave him away as a Damaron. Sin was nowhere in sight, but guards were everywhere. Hungry and with nothing else to do, she headed toward the pair on the terrace, but the other man left before she reached them.

Lion angled a lazy grin at her. "Good morning."

"Good morning." She looked after the man who had just left. "Did I interrupt you?"

"No. Wyatt had to go."

"Wyatt?"

"My cousin."

"Of course, he is. Isn't everyone?"

He chuckled. "Believe it or not, no. But I can see how it would seem that way to you at times."

She seated herself at the table and helped herself to a cup of coffee. After an experimental sip, she decided to add cream. "Have you seen Sin this morning?" She hoped the question sounded as casual as she had tried to make it, but the glint of humor in Lion's eyes told her she had not succeeded.

"He's in his office." He nodded toward her forehead. "He told me you fell. Are you feeling all right?"

"Fine." She hesitated. "Did he tell you anything else?" She reached for a spoon to stir in the cream, nonchalantly, she hoped.

"Not about you, if that's what you mean." Lion leaned back in the chair and regarded her thoughtfully. "Or you and him."

She fought against the flush she felt rising beneath her skin. After the night she had spent with Sin, she felt incredibly self-conscious, as if Sin's touch were stamped on her skin for all to see. But the question had been a stupid one and she regretted it.

"I understand Clay told you about Lily's mother."

She looked at him in surprise. "Sin told you that?"

He smiled. "No, Clay did. That boy is a talker."

Her lips quirked ruefully. "So I noticed."

"Sin never loved her, Jillian. She was dazzling, but what he and the rest of us didn't realize was that she was calculating and manipulating. She set out to deliberately trap him. He wasn't naive or completely unaware. He used protection, but it failed. And when she told him she was going to have a baby, he said he'd be there for her. That wasn't good enough for her, though. She killed herself in an effort to make him pay for not loving her."

Jillian sat very still, absorbing every word Lion said. The only thing she could think of was that he was trying to warn her away from Sin. "Why are you telling me this?"

"On the off chance that it bothers you."

She actually laughed. "Why on earth would you think that would bother me?"

"I said on the *off* chance. It was just a notion of mine."

"Don't you think a former lover of Sin's is the least of my worries?"

"I don't know. I *do* know that Sin would shoot me if he knew I talked with you about this"—he shrugged in an easygoing manner that showed he wasn't really worried about what Sin would or wouldn't do—"but I figured you and he have enough between you without this particular thing bothering you." He eyed her levelly. "I guess I don't want you to think badly of Sin."

She slowly shook her head in amazement. "You Damarons are incredible, just flat-out incredible."

A twinkle appeared in his golden eyes. "I gather that's not a compliment?"

She gestured with her hand. "All hell is about to break loose, and you care whether or not the person you're using as a pawn thinks well of your cousin."

"It's really very simple, Jillian. I care about Sin, and he cares deeply that you're going to come out of this all right. So therefore, *I* care."

She knew it was true, but she also knew something else was true. "You Damarons want it all."

"Yes," he said. "We do. And most of the time we get it."

Most of the time? From her experience it was *all* the time.

Sin . . . She longed to see him. To see how he would look at her after last night. If he would take her into his arms once again, kiss her, make love to her.

Her mind returned to what Lion had told her about Lily's mother. Last night Sin had used protection with her, but if it somehow failed and she became pregnant, he would never know. She wouldn't be able to stand his simply "being there for her." That would be intolerable to her.

She'd known his passion. She wouldn't be able to stand his indifference.

❖————————❖

The light beige carpet muffled her steps as she entered Sin's study. She'd managed to wait until after a late lunch to seek out Sin, but when he still hadn't appeared, she followed her usual pattern and went to him.

Even though she hadn't been to his study before, she'd been able to find it without too much trouble. On the other side of the house from their bedrooms, facing a different exposure, it was a paneled, sun-filled room with tan leather furniture, built-in bookshelves, and a big pecan desk. Sin was standing by the window, talking on the phone, but when he saw her, he said a few more words and hung up. He came straight to her, his eyes dark with desire, just as they had been last night.

"Hi," he said huskily, pulling her into his arms for a slow, deep kiss.

Relief flooded through her, chased by the pure pleasure of being in his arms once again. She'd intended to make light of the fact that she'd sought him out, perhaps make a joke to show that she wasn't really affected by him. But with the touch of his lips on hers, she melted, going soft and warm. "Hi," she said when she could finally draw a complete breath.

He kept her close against his hard body, with an arm around her waist. "Lord, I'm glad you came to find me. I needed to see you."

"I was in my bedroom most of the morning. Very easy to find."

"I know. I've been busy," he said softly.

"Really." She tried to pull away, but he hauled her back against him.

"Yes, really. I hated having to leave you this morning." He smiled down at her and, at the same time, ran his fingers along the side of her neck. "Do you have any idea how desirable you look when you're asleep? It was all I could do not to slide back into you while you slept and make love to you until you woke up."

The thought sent heat skidding through her veins and made her knees go weak. She wished with all her heart he'd done just that.

"Unfortunately something came up and I had to see to it."

"Something came up? You mean, while we were together? I didn't hear anything? Did someone come to the door?"

"The phone rang, but I grabbed it before it woke you."

She could believe that. In his arms, she had used up every bit of her energy, and afterward she had sunk into a deep sleep. And now she wanted to make love to him again. She pulled away from him and this time he let her go. "Have you been in here all morning?"

"Pretty much."

She spied a doll propped against a sofa pillow and covered with a doll blanket. "Heidi?"

He smiled. "Veronica. Lily was playing in here for a while and she left one of her babies to keep me company."

"She's a sweet little girl."

"Yes, she is. Thank you."

"I wondered where she was this morning. I didn't see her on the beach with Reena."

His expression turned somber. "I'm keeping her close to the house today."

Any lightness of spirit she might have been feeling disappeared. "Are you telling her why?"

"Not the entire explanation. Just that there are some bad men coming and I want to keep her safe."

"Bad men, huh?"

"It's something she can understand."

"What a shame that she has to." She spoke to herself, but he answered her.

"I agree totally."

"There ought to be a law that nothing bad can touch children until they're eighteen and able to fight back."

He smiled slowly. "I'd vote for that law."

His smile made heat crawl along her skin. After last night it was a feeling she was well familiar with. It was also a feeling she craved again. But it was a new day, and it seemed things were coming to a head. "Have you had any new word? From Steffan, I mean."

"Not directly, but yes—that's what the phone call was about." He spoke slowly. "It appears Wythe is ready to make his move. Our source says he'll be leaving the Middle East any hour now."

"Oh, God." All color drained from her skin and she sank onto the couch as the cold reality of what he had said crashed down on her.

She was worried about her stepfather, he thought, and felt an irrational surge of frustration. Irrational, because he should know better. He *did* know better.

Since he'd been given the gift of Lily, he'd come to understand how completely uncomplicated and unconditional a child's love could be. It was obviously what Jillian felt for her stepfather.

So then if he understood it, why did her concern for Wythe bother him so damned much? Why couldn't he view the matter objectively? Why did he wish she'd open her eyes and see the man for the monster he was?

He looked at Jillian again and silently called himself several choice names. He was ignoring what was important at the moment, he realized, namely, that she was very upset.

"I won't tell you again that I'm sorry for everything you've had to go through, but I will say it's almost over for you, Jillian. You'll be able to go home soon."

She wrapped her arms around her waist in an effort to warm herself. She was so cold and she felt at any minute her teeth might start chattering.

"Jillian?" He dropped down beside her and grasped her hands in his. "Jillian, what's wrong?"

"*You're* wrong."

"About what?"

"It could be just starting for me."

His forehead wrinkled in puzzlement. "I'm not sure what you're talking about. You'll be out of this soon, Jillian. Maybe as early as tomorrow."

She'd known for days that this moment would come. She'd thought about it often. But now she realized that Sin had been commanding so much of her attention that she hadn't fully faced what she would do when this time came. She forced a half laugh. "I know it's never occurred to you that Steffan could actually be successful in getting on and off this island and taking me with him, but that possibility remains."

"The odds are totally against that happening."

His confidence should have helped, but it didn't. She gave another hollow laugh. No matter how she tried, she couldn't shake her fear. There was so much Sin didn't know. But then no one knew, because she'd never been able to talk about it. "See what I mean? You won't even accept the possibility. But I have to." There was no reason to tell him about her fears now. No reason, except that she had gotten used to reaching out to him, used to having him comfort her. He was so good at it. And she felt so extraordinarily needy at the moment. "I'm afraid, Sin."

He dropped her hands. "You're afraid he won't succeed."

"No." She shook her head. "I'm afraid he will."

With a hand along her jaw, he turned her face to him. "What are you talking about, Jillian? You've got nothing to be afraid of."

She slowly shook her head. "You're wrong. You're so wrong." Telling him would accomplish nothing, she told herself. It would only serve to relieve herself of the burden of silence she'd been dealing with for years on her own. But nevertheless she was about to tell him something she had never admitted to anyone. And, in a way, having made the decision, she already felt better. "I'm afraid of Steffan. You and your family were right in your assessment that he would come to rescue me."

He nodded. "Yes, and so?"

"Put yourself in his place, Sin. *Because* he

cares so much about me, he's got to come after me. And in doing so, he will put himself in tremendous danger. And because of it—he's furious that he's been made this vulnerable. Trust me, I know him. And if he's able to get me back, he will take measures to see that nothing like this will ever happen again."

He shrugged. "I see what you're saying. He'll probably put guards on you, but bodyguards are a way of life for a lot of people."

"They can also be gotten around, taken out of action." She shook her head. "No. What he'll do is take me back to the Middle East and make sure I stay there for the rest of my life."

His expression slowly changed from one of puzzlement to one of astonishment. "You mean *against* your will?"

"That's what I mean."

She searched his face, wondering if he really, fully understood what she was saying. "The only reason I've been able to live away from him, to live on my own for as long as I have, is I very dutifully agreed to fly home every six months to see him."

Lines creased his brow. "To see him and your *mother*. You wanted to, right?"

She sighed. He didn't understand and it was so hard for her to explain. She stood up and walked over to the window. His nearness comforted her, so much so that all she wanted to do was let him hold her. But if he took her in his arms right now, she'd never be able to get the story out. "He's used my mother to keep me in a cage for years now."

"A cage?"

She glanced at him over her shoulder. "A cage. Through a series of employees, guards, if you will, he's kept a constant eye on me ever since I moved away from him. They never bothered me, not physically, anyway. But I *knew* they were there. And I always felt that at any moment they would snatch me up and take me back to him. It's one of the reasons why I moved so much. I hated being under his thumb that way, and moving was my way of trying to hide. Stupid, really, because in the end they always found me. And even though I kept my end of the bargain, to fly home every six months, more often if there was a holiday, I tried my best to be free during the interim." She wrapped her arms around herself. "And then you kidnapped me. And once again I was in a cage."

He came up behind her and pulled her back against him. "You must have thought it was Wythe who kidnapped you."

"Yes. And if it had been him, it would have meant that he'd finally snapped, something I've been afraid of for years. And if that had happened, I knew I would never know freedom again."

He fell silent, holding her against him as he tried to sort through what she had said. She was hurting and afraid and now so was he. Because he now understood that she would never love him, a man who held her in a cage against her will, no matter how gilded or comfortable that cage, when all her life she'd been trying to remain free. Sadly, even if he'd known everything ahead of time—that she feared being kept in a cage, that she would take his heart and breath away—there was nothing he could have done differently. He pressed his cheek against her silky head.

"There's more," she whispered.

"Tell me," he said, but closed his eyes almost afraid to hear.

"My mother has always been blind to Steffan's faults. She's devoted to him and thinks he's devoted to her."

"But he's not?"

"He's using her." Her voice broke, but she continued, keeping her gaze fixed firmly on the horizon. "Looking back, I think it all started before he married my mother. He became obsessed with me from the very first. Of course I didn't understand that. I only saw a man who would give me anything I wanted. He always insisted that I accompany them on their dates, which I loved, because it made me feel very grown up. My mother, of course, thought it was wonderful. They married and things continued on pretty much as they had started, with him lavishing attention and things on me. But I remember that after a while something changed and I started to shy away from him. No reason that I knew of. It was just a feeling that I didn't want to be around him. And then one night he climbed into my bed with me, waking me up."

Dread had his gut tied in knots. Keeping quiet was one of the hardest things he'd ever had to do, because he had the terrible feeling he knew what was coming, and he didn't want to hear it.

"I realize now that there had been many nights when he'd come to my room and watched me while I slept. But this night he'd been drinking enough that he got his nerve up to actually do something about his obsession. He climbed into bed with me and woke me up, woke me up from the sound sleep of an innocent child who up to that point had thought the world was all good. And I came awake to complete darkness and his hands all over me." A shudder racked her body. "It was awful. His hands were touching me everywhere. And the things he said . . ."

His hands tightened on her arms and he pressed his mouth to her ear to whisper, "God, Jillian, I'm so sorry."

"I don't know why I'm telling you this. . . ."

He turned her to face him. "I know. You want me to understand the jeopardy I've put you in, and rightly so."

"You think that's it?" She searched his face, memorizing it and the compassion she saw there. She would need to remember it in the days ahead. "I'm not sure."

"It doesn't really matter why. You're telling me and I'm glad. Go on."

She moved away from him. "The scissors—I'd been cutting out pictures from magazines, making a scrapbook." She smiled. "Not so strangely enough, I used to cut out pictures of happy families—mothers, fathers, children, all having fun together—something I guess I subconsciously yearned for."

"It's what all children yearn for."

"I was crying," she said, continuing, "screaming, scared out of my mind. I reached for the scissors and stabbed Steffan, as hard as I could, which of course wasn't very hard. I wasn't that strong at nine years old. But it was enough to stop him. The scissors went into his shoulder. As soon as he reared back to try to pull them out, I bolted off the bed and ran."

"Thank God. What happened then?"

"As twisted as he was, *is*, he didn't want me upset. From that point on, he and I had an uneasy truce, but in his own way he kept trying with me. Gifts. Attention. You name it.

My mother was ill by that time, and even as young as I was, I knew it would kill her if she found out, so I didn't tell her. I handled it and Steffan bided his time."

"That was a huge responsibility for you to carry. You were little more than a baby."

"I grew up fast. I had to. From that point on, I kept my door locked and my light on. And as soon as I was old enough, I asked to go away to school. Needless to say, he didn't want to let me go. The only thing that saved me was his self-delusion. He's always felt that someday, when I'd grown up and seen a bit of the world, I'd change my mind about him and come to love him. It was his hope, *is* to this day his hope. Sick, huh? But it's been my salvation."

"Thank God for that anyway."

"Yes. He finally agreed to let me go on the condition that I come back every six months, plus holidays. I agreed, kept up my part of the bargain, because, after all, he had my mother's well-being in his hands. There's been a subtle form of blackmail going on by both of us—each of us had something the other wanted. He wanted me and I wanted him to take care of my mother. But I never went back to live there. And as for my mother, Steffan knew that if anything happened to her, I'd be gone. So he's taken very good care of her over the years."

"The bastard." His fist opened and closed. "*I'll* kill him, if for no other reason than for just being alive all this time." He remembered wanting her to open her eyes and see Wythe for the monster he was. Now, with everything that was in him, he wished that she had been able to keep her eyes closed.

She looked at him, all her fears there in her eyes for him to see. "He's never given up, Sin. And each time I go back there . . ." She shuddered. "I won't let him get me. Even if he does get past you and your men. He's not going to get me."

"It's not going to come to that," he said grimly. "I promise you that." He held out his arms and she walked into them. He wanted to apologize to her again. He wanted to hold her close so that nothing would ever hurt her again. But most of all, he never wanted to let her go. The sheer hell of it was that now he knew for sure why he had to let her go. The knowledge should have made it easier for him. Instead, it made it harder.

"Daddy, Daddy, I need you to play with me!" Lily burst into the room, all sunshine, smiles, and blond curls, a doll cuddled in the crook of her arm. She skidded to a halt as she saw his arms around Jillian. "Hi," she said, suddenly shy.

Jillian extricated herself from Sin's arms

and took several steps away. "Hi, Lily. Did you come for your baby? Veronica?"

"Uh-huh." Her green-eyed gaze, full of curiosity, switched to her father.

He walked to her, scooped her into his arms, and kissed her baby-soft cheek. "Where's Reena?"

"I don't know," she said in a babyish sing-song voice, her gaze back on Jillian now that she was safely in her father's arms.

Just then Reena ambled into the room, serene as usual. "There you are, my little one. Ah, but you're a slippery child. She just woke up from her nap, Mr. Damaron. I turned my back and then she was gone."

"Lily," Sin said sternly, but gently. "Didn't I tell you that you were supposed to stay with Reena?"

"Uh-huh. Is Jillian playing with you?"

"Jillian and I are talking. But that's not what I asked you. Why did you slip away from Reena? I told you how important it is that you stay with her. Don't you remember?"

She nodded. "But I wanted to come see you."

"That's fine. But the next time you bring Reena with you. Okay? Tell me you understand."

"I understand."

"I hope so, because it's very important." He hugged her, then set her down, and she ran to sit on the couch beside Veronica. "Why don't you take Veronica and go back to your playroom? I'll come see you in a little bit."

She shook her head. "Come now."

"Lily—"

"Sin, don't worry about me. If you'd like to go with her, I can go back to my room. In fact that might be a good idea." She was feeling shaky and her old instinct was kicking in, the instinct to be alone, to crawl away and lick her wounds by herself.

"You can come too," Lily said, surprising the three adults in the room. "Daddy, Jillian can come, too, can't she?"

"I'd like to have a few private words with Jillian first. And then she can if she wants. But, sweetheart, I can't play right now. Remember those bad men I told you about? Well, I've got to do some things to make sure they won't hurt anyone."

She slipped off the couch, a doll in each arm. "Okay."

Jillian smiled at Lily, making an instant decision. "I'll be there in a minute."

"Hurry," Lily said.

"I will."

Sin turned to her after Lily had left with Reena. "You don't have to play with Lily if you don't feel like it."

"It'll be good for me. It'll keep me busy,

maybe keep my mind off what's happening." She doubted the last part, but it was a theory she planned to test.

"Okay, then." He reached for her and drew her into his arms. "Try not to worry. I know it's going to be next to impossible, but try anyway. And I'll try very hard not to let you down."

Let her down? she wondered. She might let herself down by wanting him more than was good for her, and by missing him when she left here. But he would never let her down, because he had never promised her anything.

TEN

It was easy for Jillian to enjoy the time she spent with Lily and to sink into the innocence of a little girl's world. But she never relaxed, and when it was time for Lily's dinner, she excused herself.

As the clock ticked the seconds away she could feel herself becoming more and more tense, and as darkness fell over the island her nerves took over and raged out of control. When Sin came to find her, she practically yelled at him.

"Where have you been? What's happening?"

"Sorry I've been so long," he said, then went straight to the point. "Wythe left the Middle East several hours ago."

Her hand pressed against her chest, right over her heart. "Where is he?"

"We don't know."

Her heart stopped, then started again with a violent thud. "What do you mean, you don't know?"

"He's out of range, both from our sources and our radar."

"No." She shook her head in rejection of what he was telling her. "That can't be. You said—"

He placed his hands on her shoulders, to reassure her, to reassure himself with the feel of her. "We never thought we'd be able to track him the whole way, Jillian. We're very good, but we're not NASA. And as he gets closer he may very well drop down and fly close to the water so that even then we won't be able to pick him up. But it's all right, because we know exactly when he left and how long it takes to make the trip from there to here. Even if he stops off for fuel or more men, which we expect him to do, we're still going to be ready for him. And most importantly, he can't get on this island without us knowing about it."

She could feel herself trembling. Willing herself to stop, she pulled away from Sin. Damn, Steffan! He had ruled her life for years, and he still had the power to frighten her senseless. "You want to hear something funny?"

He eyed her pale skin. "I doubt if I could think anything about this situation is funny."

"This *is* funny. Steffan thinks he's being a white knight, flying to my rescue, and here I am, frightened to death that he'll succeed."

"Do you think he really believes that?"

"Absolutely. I told you, he's never given up."

"Well after this, he will have no other choice but to give up. He's going to be dead or in prison."

It was so hard for her to believe that Steffan could ever lose his power to frighten her or to rule her life from afar, but she had to hold on to that thought if she was ever going to be able to make it through the coming night. "Is Lily asleep?"

He nodded. "She had such a good time with you—which I heard all about, by the way—she was worn-out."

"I had a good time too." She looked over at him. "Can you stay with me awhile?"

A muscle tightened long his jawline. "I'm not going anywhere for now. I told Lion he could find me here. Until he needs me, I'm here with you." He held out his hand, took hers, and led her to bed.

Sometime later Sin lay with Jillian, who was dozing, her back spooned against him.

It was ironic that the moment for which he had been waiting for years—the moment when the person who had killed his family was going to be brought to justice—was also going to be the moment he lost the woman he loved.

There. He'd finally admitted it to himself. *He loved her.*

He'd never fallen in love before. Never known before how a woman could get beneath his skin and fill up his heart. But she most definitely had.

And he was destined to lose her.

He was going to have to get up soon, get dressed, but he couldn't make himself just yet. He considered every moment he had left with her precious.

He wanted to imprint her body onto his so that even when she was gone he could still feel her. He wanted to brand her body with his touch so that she'd remember him always. But most of all, he never wanted to let her go.

Time was his enemy. There wasn't enough of it left. He honestly didn't think there would *ever* be enough to love her the way he wanted to. And she would never know, because she would hate it if she did.

The clock continued to tick the time away and he still couldn't make himself move. He'd never have her again, he reflected, feeling pain even as he thought it. And the more he thought about it, the more intolerable the idea became.

With a gentle hand on her shoulder, he rolled her over to him and eased into her until he couldn't go any deeper.

He had to take her one more time.

With her head resting on his broad chest, Jillian listened to the steady beat of Sin's heart. It was a soothing sound, and made her feel secure, warm, protected. But she knew this moment would soon pass and then she would be on her own again.

For most of her life she'd lived a certain way. Alone. On the move. Trying her best to be free of Steffan. It hadn't been easy, but it had worked for her.

Now, whatever the outcome of this coming clash between Sin and Steffan, her life was going to be different.

Having met Sin, having made love to him, she would never be the same. How could she be? She now knew Sin lived in the world.

The phone rang, breaking the silence and ending her languor. Before she could move, Sin's long arm reached over for the receiver. "Yes?" He listened. "I'll be right there."

She pushed herself upright, as every worry she had ever had about Steffan kicked into overdrive. "What is it?" He slammed the receiver back to its cradle, shifted off the bed, and began to dress. With his leaving, she felt an immediate loss of warmth that chilled her to her bones. "Sin, tell me."

"Two Zodiacs have been spotted offshore, one at Turquoise Cove, one across the island at Crane Cove, and two helicopters are circling the landing strip." He zipped up his pants and reached for his shirt. "This is it."

A sick feeling gripped her insides. *Steffan had come for her.* "Those places aren't very close to here, are they?"

"Not really." He looked over at her. "You ran to Turquoise Cove yesterday. In the dark, with my men everywhere, it's going to take Wythe and his men a while."

She chewed on her bottom lip. "Sounds like he's using a scattergun approach, dividing up your attention."

"That's what he's doing, but we knew he might. Given the logistical problems of attacking an island, it's an excellent tactic."

"Trust Steffan to do it right," she murmured, rubbing her arms and wondering if she'd ever feel warm again.

Finally dressed, he walked to her, his expression as grim and as serious as she'd ever seen it.

"Listen, Jillian, I need to know exactly where you are at all times, because if I do, it'll be one less worry for me. Will you promise me to stay right here?"

"Yes." It was an easy thing to promise. As it was, she felt paralyzed. She wasn't sure she'd ever be able to move again. "Sin . . . be careful."

"I will." He bent and pressed a brief kiss to her forehead. "Lock up behind me. This will all be over soon. And . . " He looked at her for several moments.

"What?"

He sighed. "Nothing. I'll be back before you know it."

She heard the door shut behind him, heard her pulse pounding in her ears, and felt cold terror twist in her stomach. Sin and his family had an island full of men, all with one intention—to capture Steffan before he could get to her.

But she wasn't reassured. Sin could have all the informants in the world, spying on Steffan, and he still wouldn't know the man as well as she did.

It didn't matter how she felt. *She had to move.* Staying immobile was the worst thing that she could do. Forcing herself, she got up and dressed, but everything she tried to do seemed to take twice as long as normal. Fear, she realized, had made her stiff and awkward. When she was at last finished, she stood in the middle of the room, unsure what to do next.

Sin had told her to lock up, but she would surely go mad if she had nothing to look at but the four walls. Plus she couldn't stand the idea of being confined, especially not with Steffan so close.

She opened the French doors and went out to the terrace. A three-quarter moon beamed high in a cloudless night sky. A mild breeze rustled through the palms. Beyond, the sea rolled toward the shore in a muted roar. It was another beautiful night in paradise and she felt very vulnerable, very alone. She could detect no movement on the grounds in front of the house.

Just then in the distance she heard shouting.

She wheeled and headed for the kitchen and the sharpest knife she could find. Back in her bedroom, she paced as she watched the clock. The knife in her hand made her feel no safer, no better, but at least she was no longer unarmed.

Except for occasional shouts she heard nothing. Lord, what had she been thinking of, promising Sin she would stay in the bedroom? She should have gone with him. He would have argued, but she could have insisted. Because if she were with him, doing whatever he was doing, she wouldn't feel like such a sitting duck.

She was tempted to go into Lily's room and climb under the covers with her, as if Lily's sweet innocence would protect her. But no, she had learned early that innocence drew evil.

Once again she returned to the terrace and scanned the grounds. She heard undistinguishable sounds in the distance. All around her, shadows lurked in the moonlight, shifting, dissolving, re-forming. Her nerves were raw and sparking, like live electric wires.

"Jillie."

Her blood ran cold, even as the world collapsed around her. *Steffan.* His harsh whisper came from her left.

Knife in hand, she whirled toward the voice. Steffan stood at the edge of the terrace, wired with adrenaline, dressed all in black. His eyes were glittering with the chilling obsession she was all too familiar with.

Smiling, he held out his hand to her. "Jillie, I've come to get you."

Suddenly she was a scared little girl again. "No."

His smile faded. "Jillie, we've got to go *now.* And good God, what are you doing with that knife? Put it down."

She saw two men behind him, *his* men, their weapons at the ready. And Steffan was holding an automatic weapon aimed at her. "You're pointing a gun at me," she said.

"What?" He looked down at the gun in his hand as if he'd forgotten he carried it. Abruptly he holstered it. "Okay, I've put it up. Let's go. We don't have much time." He held out his hand again. *"Now,* Jillie."

She swallowed, tasting bile. "I'm not going with you."

With snake-striking swiftness, his expression changed, went cold and mean. "Yes, you are." Before she could move, he stepped forward and closed his hand around her forearm, gripping her so hard she dropped the knife. "I'm here because of you. This is all your fault. If you'd stayed home where you belonged—"

Panic-stricken, she wrenched her arm away. "Leave me alone! Don't *touch* me!"

"Dammit, Jillian, now's not the time for that. We've got to get out of here. Damaron's men will be here soon. We'll talk later, but you're going home with me *now.*"

After all these years, after all the compromises and fear, after all the effort she had made to stay free, she had ended up face-to-face with Steffan in a showdown. And she'd lost her one weapon, the knife.

"For God sakes, Jillian," he said in a hiss, "your mother is waiting."

Things seemed to happen all at once. She

heard two thuds in the background and Steffan reached for her again. Revulsion and horror swept over her, strong, intense, and all-consuming. Without thinking, she grabbed his wrist and automatically her thumb found the pressure point as she had been taught long ago in one of her self-defense courses. Then she twisted his hand and he went down with a look of pain on his face.

"Jillie?" He was on his knees, his arm twisted and angled painfully upward. "What—?"

From nowhere, Sin appeared and pushed the barrel of his gun against Steffan's head. "Say the word, Jillian, and he'll be out of your life forever."

The world was suddenly quiet and still, its scope narrowed down to Steffan's pale, shocked face. She'd overcome him, she realized with astonishment, and she hadn't needed the knife after all. She'd been able to use her weight and balance against him, and, at last he was at her mercy.

"Jillian, I've got him now. You can let his arm go."

But she couldn't. It felt too good to have him on his knees, feeling pain she was inflicting.

Steffan cursed. "Damaron, damn you, you're going to pay for this!"

Sin ignored him, still concentrating on Jillian. "Say the word. What do you want?"

Tears stung her eyes, sweat beaded her face and body, her breath came in gasps. She wanted Steffan dead. She wanted it so badly she could taste it.

"Jillian, don't listen to him!"

Time was crawling and going by faster all at once. She saw Steffan's two men lying on the ground just beyond them, and she saw Damaron guards standing over them. Sin was giving her the opportunity to get Steffan out of her life once and for all. She was going to take it. She dropped Steffan's arm and stepped away. "No."

"No, what?"

"I don't want to kill him. I don't want him to die. I want him to go to prison for what he's done. I want him to be in a cage for the rest of his life, just like I've been up until now."

"Jillie! For God's sake, what are you saying?"

She looked down at Steffan one last time. If she ever thought of him again—and she was going to try not to—she wanted to remember him this way, frightened, hurting, but most of all helpless, just as she had been on that long-ago night when he'd crawled into bed with her. "I'm saying good-bye, Steffan. Once and for all. *Forever.*"

"No, no. This has all been a *shock* for you. You don't know what you're doing!"

His capacity for self-delusion amazed her. "I know exactly what I'm doing."

"No! Listen to me! Even if Damaron sees to it that I'm put in prison, I'll get out. Don't worry about that."

"I'm not. Not at all." She lifted her gaze to Sin, knowing with absolute certainty that he and his family were going to see to it that Steffan was put away for the rest of his life. She'd never have to worry about Steffan again. She'd taken him to his knees and now Sin was going to put him in a cage. "Goodbye," she said, feeling a type of peace she'd never felt before. He uttered a string of curses, mixing them with heartfelt entreaties, but she didn't care. She walked into her room and shut the door.

Sometime later, as the dawn was breaking in pearl-colored layers over the island, her bedroom door opened and Sin strode in. Without preamble, he hauled her into his arms. "God, I'm so sorry that he got to you. It was the very last thing I wanted to happen."

She closed her eyes, savoring the strength of his arms around her. It seemed like forever since she had felt them. In reality, it had been mere hours. "It doesn't matter."

"To me it does."

"Don't let it." Reluctantly she pulled away. "It had to happen."

"No. No, it didn't." Anger still simmered in his tense body. "I should have gotten to him before he got to you. And I damn sure should have blown him away."

He took her face between his hands and stared deeply into her eyes. "Tell me you're all right."

"I am. I really am." She laughed and was startled to hear the humor, strained though it was. "I feel as if I've lost a hundred pounds. I had no idea that anger and fear can be such a heavy burden."

"I can sure as hell testify to anger," he said shakily. "I would be feeling a lot better right now if I'd killed him."

"No." She reached out and caressed his face, for the first time comforting him. "You don't want that sin on your soul. In the end, I didn't either."

He exhaled heavily. "That's the one thing I'm happy about. You've had to live with too much as it is."

"Where is he?"

"Gone. They all are. As we speak, Wythe is being flown to New York, where the authorities are waiting for him. Two of my cousins are accompanying him. The men who came with him are on their way back to the

Middle East. We had no quarrel with them, and despite what just occurred, we have no wish to start a war."

She clasped her hands together. "So that's it. You've finally gotten your revenge for the death of your family."

"Yes."

"And do you think you'll be able to rest easier now that you have?"

He nodded. "About Wythe, I will—most definitely."

"That's good. I'm glad."

He nodded, folding his arms across his chest as he studied her. There was so much he wanted to say to her, so much he couldn't let himself say. But in the end, there was one thing he couldn't keep to himself. "I'll tell you what's not so good. The fact that you won't be coming to my room at night anymore. I'm not sure I'll be able to get any rest."

"I hope that's not true." She could see the desire in his eyes, hear it in his voice. And she couldn't cope with it. Not now. He absorbed the flatness of her tone and felt defeated. She'd been put through a wringer, and all because of something that had had nothing to do with her. He wanted nothing more than to help her. There was so much he had power over, so much he could do for her if she'd only let him. "Your mother," he said. "What are you going to do about her?"

"Bring her back to the States. Check her into a good hospital."

"Has it occurred to you that Steffan might have been giving her drugs, keeping her just sick enough that you'd have to keep coming back."

"Yes, it's occurred to me. More than once, but I was never in a position to do anything about it. Now I am, and once and for all I can find out what's wrong with her. Thank you for that."

He smiled grimly. "Sure." Then hope sparked in him. "You're going to need money. Let me give you that."

She shook her head. "Steffan has been putting money in a special account for me for years. Up until now I haven't touched a penny of it. Now I will. For Mom. I figure it's only right."

There was one more thing he could try to do for her, he realized. He handed her a card. "No matter where I am, you can reach me through this number. Promise me you'll call if you need anything, anything at all."

She stared down at the card, unable to see the numbers for the tears sheening her eyes. It seemed leaving was going to be twice as painful as being brought here had been. "Will you be staying on this island?"

"No, Lily and I will be flying back to New York within a few hours. She's in a play group there that she really likes, and I have to get back to business as usual." He paused, searching his mind for something else he could say that might make a difference between them, might make her stay with him, might make her accept his help. But he couldn't come up with a thing. "Are you ready to leave now?"

"I'd like to say good-bye to Lily first."

Jillian found Lily on the beach, carrying a pail full of odds and ends that she'd picked up that morning. Reena was watching from her perch on a rock a few yards away.

Lily was back on the beach, Jillian thought, and all was right with the world.

As she approached, Lily looked up at her and gave her a sweet smile. "Hi."

"Hi, Lily."

"Have you come to play with me?"

"No, honey, I've come to say good-bye."

"Why?"

Good question, she thought wryly. It wasn't as if she had a real life back in Maine, or anywhere else for that matter. But nevertheless she had to go. She knelt in the sand in front of Lily so that she was at eye level with her. "I need to go home."

"Uh-uh." Lily swung her small body back

and forth—her way of shaking her head. "You can stay here with me and Daddy. Daddy likes you."

Jillian smiled. If only life were as simple as Lily thought it was. "I'm sorry, but I've got to go, sweetheart." Tears welled in the little girl's eyes, making them luminous. Unable to help herself, she hugged Lily to her. "Don't cry, Lily. Your daddy told me you're going back to your home in New York. Your play group will be there."

Lily's gaze was solemn. "I think they probably miss me. Kirby too."

"Your dog?" With a light laugh, Jillian said, "I think you're right." She hugged her one more time, then stood and headed back to the house.

Sin was waiting for her on the main terrace.

He looked at her. "I've got to let you go. I know that. I'm just not sure I can."

She had never felt less like smiling, but she did. "I guess I'm ready." Funny, she felt like thanking him, as if for the last week she'd been an ordinary house guest. And in more ways than one he *did* deserve her thanks. Thanks to him, Steffan would never bother her again. Sin had given her the gift of freedom.

"I'm *not* ready for you to go," he told her. "But you'll let me go, because you told me that you would. After all, you're an honorable man. Clay told me, remember?"

"Then I guess I have no choice. The jet will be ready when you are. Lion will accompany you home."

"That's not necessary."

"He thinks it is. And besides . . ."

"Besides?"

"He doesn't trust me to do it, and I don't either."

His green eyes blazed with a glittering fire that warned her of what was coming next.

"I may decide to kidnap you again and this time not let you go."

As always, she believed him.

Everything was the same, Jillian thought, standing on the rugged, untamed beach in Maine, feeling the wind against her face, tasting the salt on her lips, seeing the waves crash to shore. Maine was the same. The beach was the same. Life went on around her the same way. But she was changed.

Jimmy had hired someone else to take her place, but softhearted and gregarious as always, he offered her old job back to her, unworried that there might not be enough work for an extra waitress. She'd declined.

She was free now. As free as the wind, the sea, the birds. It was a heady, sparkling feeling. She no longer had to look over her shoulder for Steffan's men, no longer had to fear that Steffan would one day snap and take her to the Middle East against her will.

Her mother was now being treated in New York in one of the best hospitals in the country. A battery of tests were being run, and the doctors were optimistic. Whatever the results of the tests, Jillian believed with all her heart that her mother was infinitely better off.

She'd been understandably and predictably upset to learn that Steffan was in prison. But Jillian hoped that once the matter of her health was settled, she would come to understand at least a part of what had happened. Jillian might never tell her everything, but it was her hope that they could eventually forge a new and warm relationship.

In the meantime she had to decide what she was going to do with the rest of her life. The world was open before her. She had her mother back. She had all the money in the world.

But she was unhappy, heartsick, lonely . . . for Sin.

It had been three weeks since she had seen him, three weeks since she had felt his touch, three weeks since . . .

She loved him. She didn't know how it had happened or when it had happened, but she loved him. It flew against all reason, all logic, but she loved him.

She loved him with all her heart.

She just wasn't sure what she was going to do about it.

And then it came to her.

She saw him, sitting on the very same out-cropping of rocks he had sat on a month ago, staring out at the sea. The sun had just set. There wasn't a cloud in the sky. And thankfully the storm was over.

And this time, before she looked into his eyes, she knew they were going to be the beautiful color of dark jade.

She hadn't been afraid that first time she'd seen him, and she wasn't afraid this time, either. But she *was* apprehensive.

He turned his head and, as soon as he saw her, stood. "Hello." He studied her anxiously. "How are you?"

Butterflies filled her stomach. She clasped her hands together and felt the dampness on her palms. She knew what she wanted to say to him, but she was unsure how she was going to tell him or even what his reaction would be. "I'm fine. How's Lily?"

"She's well. She still talks about you."

"Does she?" She smiled in spite of her nervousness.

He nodded, his gaze going to her lips, then back to her face. "Your message said you wanted to see me. No reason. Just the time and the place. I've been very worried that something was wrong."

"Nothing's wrong. I just wanted to see you." He looked the same, she thought, hungrily gazing at him. He hadn't lost one iota of his power and appeal.

He reached out a tentative hand and touched her hair. "You're all right? I mean you're *really* all right?"

"Yes, I really am. And I guess since you didn't know, it means you haven't had me watched." She'd meant to tease, but somehow her words came out sounding more serious than she had intended.

"I wouldn't do that to you again."

"I—I knew that. I didn't mean—"

"I'm glad you contacted me, Jillian. I've been going crazy, wondering how you were."

"Things have been going well. Very well. Except, I really wanted to see you." Feeling tongue-tied, she laughed self-consciously. "I thought about staging a mock kidnapping."

"You don't have to do that. I'll go anywhere you want."

Her heart lurched. "You're being very serious."

"And you're making me very nervous."

She shrugged. "I'm sorry. I have something I need to tell you, and I'm just anxious about how you're going to take it."

He tried to imagine what she had to say to him that would make her anxious. But all he could concentrate on was what he needed to say to her, what he *should* have said to her three weeks ago. The words had been all jammed up in him then, but now they came tumbling out. "I love you, Jillian. I've been miserable without you. If you hadn't contacted me I'm not sure how long I could have held out without finding out where you were and coming to see you."

She heard only the first part of what he said. Her mind had stopped with *I love you.* "You love me?"

A shudder went through him. He'd thought that just seeing her would be enough for him. But it wasn't. He wanted to touch her, kiss her, but he was afraid that if he started he wouldn't be able to stop, no matter what she said. So he stood there, with his hands in his pockets, aching in every part of his body for her. "I love you so much, I let you go. And I've regretted it ever since. It was the right thing to do for you, but it couldn't have been more wrong for me. I—"

She held up her hand. "Wait. Stop." Her mind was having trouble assimilating everything. "Before you say anything else, let me talk."

His hands came out of his pockets and were halfway to her when he caught himself and pulled them back. "If you're going to tell me to leave, don't. I wouldn't be able to take it."

Happiness bubbled inside her, along with a hope for the future. Hope and happiness were so new to her, she was afraid they'd vanish if she didn't take control of what was happening. "I love you, Sin. That's what I want to say to you. I *love* you. But I had to leave you and get off that island before I was able to realize it. I had to be free before I could see you again."

He went still, but his eyes gleamed with a heated darkness. "Be very, very sure, Jillian, of what you're saying. I let you go once. I'll never do it again."

She couldn't suppress her laugh of sheer joy, and she threaded her arms around his neck. "Considering that you kidnapped me, the proper thing to say to me would be that I'll always be free to leave."

"But you won't," he said gruffly, pulling her against him. "And you need to know that. Because once we're married, you'll never get away from me. You will have lost your chance of ever being free of me again. I simply wouldn't be able to take it if you walked out on me."

"Married?" Now it was her turn to go

still. Strangely enough she had never considered marriage. That, she realized, would bind her to Sin for the rest of her life. But then wasn't that what love was all about? And she did love him.

Silently he cursed. "I've frightened you. I'm sorry. I didn't mean to." He pressed his lips to her head, then eased away from her so that he could see her face. "The last few weeks have been hell without you."

She understood. She hadn't been able to get him out of her mind for a minute. She'd asked him here so that she could tell him that she loved him with everything that was in her. She'd hoped against hope that he would tell her the same. He had, then had taken one step further by revealing he wanted to marry her.

Nothing he had said had changed a thing, she realized. She had the power. She had the freedom to accept or deny, to choose to marry him or not. And the truth was she didn't want to be free from him.

She looked up at him, her eyes sparkling with love. "Yes, Sin, I'll marry you."

He hadn't asked her, he realized. He'd simply assumed. It wasn't like him, but then he had never before loved the way that he loved her. "Thank you," he said softly.

"Thank *you*," she whispered back, happier than she had ever been. Because she now understood that in loving Sin, she would gain a new kind of freedom. The freedom to put aside all the old nightmares and to fix her sights on a future that would be filled with love and laughter, joy and passion. "I'm going to spend the rest of my life with you," she said, "and I want to start right now."

With a gruff sound, he pulled her into his arms and began a kiss that would stretch over a lifetime, with barely a pause in between.

THE EDITORS' CORNER

Fall is just around the corner, but there's one way you can avoid the chill in the air. Cuddle up with the LOVESWEPT novels coming your way next month. These heart-melting tales of romance are guaranteed to keep you warm with the heat of passion.

Longtime LOVESWEPT favorite Peggy Webb returns with a richly emotional tale of forbidden desire in **INDISCREET**, LOVESWEPT #802. Bolton Gray Wolf appears every inch a savage when he arrives to interview Virginia Haven, but the moment she rides up on a white Arabian stallion, challenge glittering in her eyes, he knows he will make her his! Even as his gaze leaves her breathless, Virginia vows he'll never tame her; but once they touch, she has no choice but to surrender. Peggy Webb offers a spectacular glimpse into the astonishing mysteries of love in a tale of fiery magic and unexpected miracles.

Marcia Evanick delivers her award-winning blend of love and laughter in **SECOND-TIME LUCKY**, LOVESWEPT #803. Luke Callahan arrives without warning to claim a place in Dayna's life, but he reminds her too much of the heartbreak she'd endured during her marriage to his brother! Luke wants to help raise her sons, but even more, he wants the woman he's secretly loved for years. Dared by his touch, drawn by his warmth to open her heart, Dayna feels her secret hopes grow strong. In a novel that explores the soul-deep hunger of longing and loneliness, Marcia Evanick weaves a wonderful tapestry of emotion and humor, dark secrets and tender joys.

A love too long denied finds a second chance in **DESTINY STRIKES TWICE**, LOVESWEPT #804, by Maris Soule. Effie Sanders returns to the lake to pack up her grandmother's house and the memory of summers spent tagging along with her sister Bernadette . . . and Parker Morgan. With his blue eyes and lean, tanned muscles, Parker had always been out of Effie's reach, had never noticed her in the shadow of her glamorous sister. Never—until an older, overworked Parker comes to his family's cottage to learn to relax and finds the irrepressible girl he once knew has grown up to become a curvy, alluring woman. And suddenly he is anything but relaxed. Maris Soule has created a story that ignites with fiery desire and ripples with tender emotion.

And finally, Faye Hughes gives the green light to scandal in **LICENSED TO SIN**, LOVESWEPT #805. In a voice so sensual it makes her toes curl, Nick Valdez invites Jane Steele to confess her secrets, making her fear that her cover has been blown! But she knows she's safe when the handsome gambler then suggests they join forces to investigate rigged games at a riverboat casino. She agrees to his scheme, knowing that sharing close quarters with Nick will be risky temptation. In this blend of steamy romance and fast-paced adventure, Faye Hughes reveals the tantalizing pleasures of playing dangerous games and betting it all on the roll of the dice.

Happy reading!

With warmest wishes,

Beth de Guzman

Shauna Summers

Beth de Guzman

Shauna Summers

Senior Editor

Editor

P.S. Watch for these Bantam women's fiction titles coming in September. With her mesmerizing voice and spellbinding touch of contemporary romantic suspense, Kay Hooper wowed readers and reviewers alike with her Bantam hardcover debut, **AMANDA**—and it's soon coming your way in paperback. Nationally bestselling author Patricia Potter shows her flair for humor and warm emotion in **THE MARSHAL AND THE HEIRESS**; this one has a western lawman lassoing the bad guys all the way in Scotland! From Adrienne deWolfe, the author *Ro-*

mantic Times hailed as "an exciting new talent," comes **TEXAS LOVER,** the enthralling tale of a Texas Ranger, a beautiful Yankee woman, and a houseful of orphans. Be sure to see next month's LOVESWEPTs for a preview of these exceptional novels. And immediately following this page, preview the Bantam women's fiction titles on sale *now*!

Don't miss these extraordinary books
by your favorite Bantam authors

On sale in July:

PRINCE OF SHADOWS
by Susan Krinard

WALKING RAIN
by Susan Wade

No one could tame him. Except a woman
in love.

From the electrifying talent of

Susan Krinard

author of *Star-Crossed* and *Prince of Wolves*
comes a breathtaking, magical new
romance

PRINCE OF SHADOWS

"Susan Krinard has set the standard for
today's fantasy romance."—*Affaire de Coeur*

*Scarred by a tragic accident, Alexandra Warrington has
come back to the Minnesota woods looking for refuge and a
chance to carry on her passionate study of wolves. But her
peace is shattered when she awakes one morning to find a
total stranger in her bed. Magnificently muscled and perfectly naked, he exudes a wildness that frightens her and a
haunting fear that touches her. Yet Alex doesn't realize
that this handsome savage is a creature out of myth, a wolf
transformed into a man. And when the town condemns
him for a terrible crime, all she knows is that she is dan-
gerously close to loving him and perilously committed to
saving him . . . no matter what the cost.*

The wolf was on his feet again, standing by the door.
She forgot her resolve not to stare. Magnificent was
the only word for him, even as shaky as he was. He

lifted one paw and scraped it against the door, turning to look at her in a way that couldn't be misunderstood.

He wanted out. Alex felt a sudden, inexplicable panic. He wasn't ready. Only moments before she'd been debating what to do with him, and now her decision was being forced.

Once she opened that door he'd be gone, obeying instincts older and more powerful than the ephemeral trust he'd given her on the edge of death. In his weakened state, once back in the woods he'd search out the easiest prey he could find.

Livestock. Man's possessions, lethally guarded by guns and poison.

Alex backed away, toward the hall closet, where she kept her seldom-used dart gun. In Canada she and her fellow researchers had used guns like it to capture wolves for collaring and transfer to new homes in the northern United States. She hadn't expected to need it here.

Now she didn't have any choice. Shadow leaned against the wall patiently as she retrieved the gun and loaded it out of his sight. She tucked it into the loose waistband of her jeans, at the small of her back, and started toward the door.

Shadow wagged his tail. Only once, and slowly, but the simple gesture cut her to the heart. It was as if he saw her as another wolf. As if he recognized what she'd tried to do for him. She edged to the opposite side of the door and opened it.

Biting air swirled into the warmth of the cabin. Shadow stepped out, lifting his muzzle to the sky, breathing in a thousand subtle scents Alex couldn't begin to imagine.

She followed him and sat at the edge of the porch

as he walked stiffly into the clearing. "What are you?" she murmured. "Were you captive once? Were you cut off from your own kind?"

He heard her, pausing in his business and pricking his ears. Golden eyes held answers she couldn't interpret with mere human senses.

"I know what you aren't, Shadow. You aren't meant to be anyone's pet. Or something to be kept in a cage and stared at. I wish to God I could let you go."

The wolf whuffed softly. He looked toward the forest, and Alex stiffened, reaching for the dart gun. But he turned back and came to her again, lifted his paw and set it very deliberately on her knee.

Needing her. Trusting her. Accepting. His huge paw felt warm and familiar, like a friend's touch.

Once she'd loved being touched. By her mother, by her grandparents—by Peter. She'd fought so hard to get over that need, that weakness.

Alex raised her hand and felt it tremble. She let her fingers brush the wolf's thick ruff, stroke down along his massive shoulder. Shadow sighed and closed his eyes to slits of contentment.

Oh, God. In a minute she'd be flinging her arms around his great shaggy neck. *Wrong, wrong.* He was a wolf, not a pet dog. She withdrew her hands and clasped them in her lap.

He nudged her hand. His eyes, amber and intelligent, regarded her without deception. Like no human eyes in the world.

"I won't let them kill you, Shadow," she said hoarsely. "No matter what you are, or what happens. I'll help you. I promise." She closed her eyes. "I've made promises I wasn't able to keep, but not this time. Not this time."

Promises. One to a strange, lost boy weeping over the bodies of two murdered wolves. A boy who, like the first Shadow, she'd never found again.

And another promise to her mother, who had died to save her.

The ghost of one had returned to her at last.

The wolf whined and patted her knee, his claws snagging on her jeans. A gentle snow began to fall, thick wet flakes that kissed Alex's cheeks with the sweetness of a lover. She turned her face up to the sky's caress. Shadow leaned against her heavily, his black pelt dusted with snowflakes.

If only I could go back, she thought. Back to the time when happiness had been such a simple thing, when a wolf could be a friend and fairy tales were real. She sank her fingers deeper into Shadow's fur.

If only—you were human. A man as loyal, as protective, as fundamentally honest as a wolf with its own. A man who could never exist in the real world. A fairy-tale hero, a prince ensorcelled.

She allowed herself a bitter smile. The exact opposite of Peter, in fact.

And you think you'd deserve such a man, if he did exist?

She killed that line of thought before it could take hold, forcing her fingers to unclench from Shadow's fur. "What am I going to do, Shadow?" she said.

The wolf set his forepaws on the porch and heaved his body up, struggling to lift himself to the low platform. Alex watched his efforts with a last grasp at objectivity.

Now. Dart him now, and there will still be time to contact the ADC. She clawed at the dart gun and pulled it from her waistband.

But Shadow looked up at her in that precise moment, and she was lost. "I can't," she whispered. She let her arm go slack. The dart gun fell from her nerveless fingers, landing in the snow. She stared at it blindly.

Teeth that could rend and tear so efficiently closed with utmost gentleness around her empty hand. Shadow tugged until she had no choice but to look at him again.

She knew what he wanted. She hesitated only a moment before opening the door. Shadow padded into the cabin and found the place she had made for him by the stove, stretching out full-length on the old braided rug, chin on paws.

"You've made it easy for me, haven't you?" she asked him, closing the door behind her. "You're trapped, and I can keep you here until . . . until I can figure out what to do with you."

The wolf gazed at her so steadily that she was almost certain that he'd known exactly what he was doing. She wanted to go to him and huddle close, feel the warmth of his great body and the sumptuous texture of his fur. But she had risked too much already. In the morning she'd have to reach a decision about him, and she knew how this would end—how it must end—sooner or later.

Shadow would be gone, and she'd be alone.

Feeling decades older than her twenty-seven years, Alex took her journal from the kitchen and retreated into the darkness of her bedroom. She paused at the door, her hand on the knob, and closed it with firm and deliberate pressure.

She stripped off her clothes and hung them neatly in the tiny closet, retrieving a clean pair of long underwear. The journal lay open on the old wooden bed table, waiting for the night's final entry.

It's ironic, Mother. I thought I'd become strong. Objective. I can't even succeed in this.

Her flannel bedsheets were cold; she drew the blankets up high around her chin, an old childhood habit she'd never shaken. Once it had made her feel safe, as if her mother's own hands had tucked her in. Now it only made her remember how false a comfort it truly was.

It was a long time before she slept. The sun was streaming through the curtains when she woke again. She lay very still, cherishing the ephemeral happiness that came to her at the very edge of waking.

She wasn't alone. There was warmth behind her on the bed, a familiar weight at her back that pulled down the mattress. The pressure of another body, masculine and solid.

Peter. She kept her eyes closed. It wasn't often that Peter slept the night through and was still beside her when she woke. And when he was . . .

His hand brushed her hip, hot through the knit fabric of her long underwear. When Peter was with her in the morning, it was because he wanted to make love. She gasped silently as his palm moved down to the upper edge of her thigh and then back up again, drawing the hem of her top up and up until he found skin.

Alex shuddered. It had been so long. Her belly tightened in anticipation. Peter wanted her. He *wanted* her. His fingers stroked along her ribs with delicate tenderness. They brushed the lower edge of her breast. Her nipples hardened almost painfully.

The arousal was a release, running hot in her blood. In a moment she would roll over and into his arms. In a moment she'd give herself up to the sex, to the searing intensity of physical closeness, seizing it for as long as it lasted.

But for now Peter was caressing her gently, without his usual impatience—taking time to make her ready, to feed her excitement—and she savored it. She wouldn't ruin the moment with words. Peter wasn't usually so silent. He liked talking before and after making love. About his plans, his ambitions. Their future.

All she could hear of him now was his breathing, sonorous and steady. His palm rested at the curve of her waist, the fingers making small circles on her skin.

His fingers. Callused fingers. She could feel their slight roughness. Blunt at the tips, not tapered. Big hands.

Big hands. Too big.

Wrongness washed through her in a wave of adrenaline. She snapped open her eyes and stared at the cracked face of the old-fashioned alarm clock beside the bed. Granddad's alarm clock. And beyond, the wood plank walls of the cabin.

Not the apartment. Her cabin. Not the king-size bed but her slightly sprung double.

The hand at her waist stilled.

Alex jerked her legs and found them trapped under an implacable weight. A guttural, groaning sigh sounded in her ear.

Very slowly she turned her head.

A man lay beside her, sprawled across the bed with one leg pinning the blankets over hers. A perfectly naked, magnificently muscled stranger. His body was curled toward her, head resting on one arm. His other hand was on her skin. Straight, thick black hair shadowed his face.

Alex did no more than tense her body, but that was enough. The man moved; the muscles of his torso and flat belly rippled as he stretched and lifted his head. Yellow eyes met her gaze through the veil of his hair.

Yellow eyes. Clear as sunlight, fathomless as ancient amber. Eyes that almost stopped her heart.

For an instant—one wayward, crazy instant—Alex *knew* him. And then that bizarre sensation passed to be replaced with far more pragmatic instincts. She twisted and bucked to free her legs and shoved him violently, knocking his hand from her body. His eyes widened as he rocked backward on the narrow bed, clawed at the sheets and rolled over the far edge.

Alex tore the covers away and leaped from the bed, remembering belatedly that she'd left the dart gun outside, and Granddad's old rifle was firmly locked away in the hall closet. She spun for the door just as the man scrambled to his feet, tossing the hair from his eyes. Her hand had barely touched the doorknob when he lunged across the bed and grabbed her wrist in an iron grip.

Treacherous terror surged in her. She lashed out, and he caught her other hand. She stared at the man with his strange, piercing eyes and remembered she was not truly alone.

A wolf slept just beyond her door. A wolf that had trusted and accepted her as if she were a member of his pack. One of his own kind. A wolf that seemed to recognize the name she had given him.

"Shadow," she cried. It came out as a whisper. "Shadow!"

The man twitched. The muscles of his strong jaw stood out in sharp relief beneath tanned skin, and his fingers loosened around her wrists for one vital instant.

Alex didn't think. She ripped her arms free of his grasp, clasped her hands into a single fist, and struck him with all her strength.

Haunting, compelling, and richly atmospheric, this dazzling novel of romantic suspense marks the impressive debut of a talented new author.

WALKING RAIN

by Susan Wade

Eight years with a new name and a new identity had not succeeded in wiping out the horrors of the past. It was time for Amelia Rawlins to go home. Home to the New Mexico ranch where she had spent her childhood summers. Home to the place where she could feel her grandfather's spirit and carry on the work he had loved. But someone knew that Amelia had come back—Amelia, who should have died on that long-ago day . . . who should have known better than to think she could come back and start over with nothing more than a potter's wheel, a handful of wildflower seeds, and a stubborn streak. And someone was out to see that Amelia paid in full for her crimes. . . .

She drove up U.S. 54 from Interstate 10 because that was the way she had always come to the ranch. Her old pickup had held up well on the long drive from the East Coast, but now it rattled and jounced along the battered road. Amelia checked the rearview mirror often, making certain her potter's wheel was still securely lashed to the bed of the truck. It was her habit to watch her back.

She'd reached El Paso late in the afternoon and

stopped there to put gas in the truck. Between that stop and all the Juarez traffic, it was getting on toward evening by the time she left the city and, with it, the interstate. Now the mountains of the Tularosa basin rose on either side of the two-lane road: the soaring ridge of the Guadalupes to her east and the Organ Mountains, drier, more distant, to her west. The eastern range was heavily snowed, peaks gleaming pink in the fading light, and the evening sky was winter-brilliant. Narrow bands of clouds glowed like flamingo feathers above the Organs.

She had forgotten the crystalline stillness of the air here, forgotten the sunny chill of a New Mexico winter. How had that happened? Maybe that was the price she'd paid for forgetting the things she had to forget. Part of the price.

The sun flamed on the horizon, looking as if it would flow down the mountains to melt the world, and then it sank. Its light faded quickly from the sky; already the stars were taking their turn at ruling the deep blue reaches. Amelia rolled down her window, even though the temperature outside was plunging toward freezing. The desert smelled pungent and strong, and there was a hint of pine and piñon on the wind.

It was the wind that whipped tears to her eyes. Certainly the wind; she was not a woman who wept. But she was suddenly swept by a brilliant ache of homesickness—here, now, when she was very near the only home left to her—it caught at her violently. So violently that she almost turned the truck around and went away again.

To need something so much frightened her.

But she was tired, and she had only decided to come here when she could no longer face starting over somewhere new. She'd been rootless for too long.

So the truck spun on, winding north in the star-studded darkness, past the ghostly dunes of White Sands, north and then eventually east, to a narrower road, one that ran deep into the wrinkled land at the foot of the Guadalupes.

She made her way to the Crossroads by feel, and turned left without thinking. It was unsettling to be in a place so instantly familiar. The stars had come full out; the desert was bright beneath them. An ancient seabed, the Tularosa basin was now four thousand feet above sea level, and the air was thin, rarefied, so the starlight streamed through it undiminished. Amelia could see the beacon of the observatory to the south, high on the mountain, gleaming like a fallen star itself.

And then she was there, bumping the truck off the road next to the dirt lane that led to the house. The gate was closed. A new gate, one of those metal-barred affairs. Amelia left the truck idling when she got out, not sure it would start again if she turned it off after such a long run. But when she tried to open the gate, she found it padlocked. Her grandfather never did that.

She climbed up on the gate and looked toward the ranch house, sprawling among the cottonwood trees beyond the fields. No lights. No smoke from the chimney pipe. The windows were dark vacant blanks against the pale adobe walls of the house. She could see the looming windmill, its blades turning slowly in silhouette, but nothing else moved.

So maybe the ranch hadn't been leased to someone else. Maybe her uncle hadn't decided she was dead and sold the place off. Maybe none of the things she'd been afraid of had happened.

She should have been relieved. But the homesickness was back, wilder than ever, and she realized that some part of her had expected her grandfather to be there waiting for her.

He was dead. Bound to be. He'd been seventy-six the last time she and her kid brother had come for the summer, and that was more than a dozen years ago. But one thing she had no doubt about—that Gramps had kept his word and left the property to her. She knew he had, as surely as she knew the pattern the cottonwoods' shadow would paint on the house in summer. This place was part of her.

She went back and cut off the truck. The silence was a living one, even in February. The rustle of a mouse in its nest and the faraway cry of a hunting night bird gathered on the wind. Amelia shivered. She put on her down vest, then took her backpack and her cooler out of the truck. Nobody would bother her things, not out here. Gramps used to say they could go a week without seeing another soul on this road.

He'd been exaggerating, of course. Something he was prone to. Amelia dropped the cooler over the fence, then swung herself over the gate. She picked up the cooler and started down the lane toward the house. The smell of the desert seemed even more sharply familiar now, thick with memories. She remembered racing Michael down this road on bikes—Gramps taking the two of them to collect native grasses by the old railroad tracks, Gramma baking biscuits in the cool of the morning. So many memories. A cascade of them.

They were falling around her like rain. Amelia bowed her head and walked up the road into it.

On sale in August:

AMANDA
by Kay Hooper

THE MARSHAL AND THE HEIRESS
by Patricia Potter

TEXAS LOVER
by Adrienne deWolfe

To enter the sweepstakes outlined below, you must respond by the date specified and follow all entry instructions published elsewhere in this offer.

DREAM COME TRUE SWEEPSTAKES

Sweepstakes begins 9/1/94, ends 1/15/96. To qualify for the Early Bird Prize, entry must be received by the date specified elsewhere in this offer. Winners will be selected in random drawings on 2/29/96 by an independent judging organization whose decisions are final. Early Bird winner will be selected in a separate drawing from among all qualifying entries.

Odds of winning determined by total number of entries received. Distribution not to exceed 300 million.

Estimated maximum retail value of prizes: Grand (1) $25,000 (cash alternative $20,000); First (1) $2,000; Second (1) $750; Third (50) $75; Fourth (1,000) $50; Early Bird (1) $5,000. Total prize value: $86,500.

Automobile and travel trailer must be picked up at a local dealer; all other merchandise prizes will be shipped to winners. Awarding of any prize to a minor will require written permission of parent/guardian. If a trip prize is won by a minor, s/he must be accompanied by parent/legal guardian. Trip prizes subject to availability and must be completed within 12 months of date awarded. Blackout dates may apply. Early Bird trip is on a space available basis and does not include port charges, gratuities, optional shore excursions and onboard personal purchases. Prizes are not transferable or redeemable for cash except as specified. No substitution for prizes except as necessary due to unavailability. Travel trailer and/or automobile license and registration fees are winners' responsibility as are any other incidental expenses not specified herein.

Early Bird Prize may not be offered in some presentations of this sweepstakes. Grand through third prize winners will have the option of selecting any prize offered at level won. All prizes will be awarded. Drawing will be held at 204 Center Square Road, Bridgeport, NJ 08014. Winners need not be present. For winners list (available in June, 1996), send a self-addressed, stamped envelope by 1/15/96 to: Dream Come True Winners, P.O. Box 572, Gibbstown, NJ 08027.

THE FOLLOWING APPLIES TO THE SWEEPSTAKES ABOVE:

No purchase necessary. No photocopied or mechanically reproduced entries will be accepted. Not responsible for lost, late, misdirected, damaged, incomplete, illegible, or postage-die mail. Entries become the property of sponsors and will not be returned.

Winner(s) will be notified by mail. Winner(s) may be required to sign and return an affidavit of eligibility/release within 14 days of date on notification or an alternate may be selected. Except where prohibited by law entry constitutes permission to use of winners' names, hometowns, and likenesses for publicity without additional compensation. Void where prohibited or restricted. All federal, state, provincial, and local laws and regulations apply.

All prize values are in U.S. currency. Presentation of prizes may vary; values at a given prize level will be approximately the same. All taxes are winners' responsibility.

Canadian residents, in order to win, must first correctly answer a time-limited skill testing question administered by mail. Any litigation regarding the conduct and awarding of a prize in this publicity contest by a resident of the province of Quebec may be submitted to the Regie des loteries et courses du Quebec.

Sweepstakes is open to legal residents of the U.S., Canada, and Europe (in those areas where made available) who have received this offer.

Sweepstakes in sponsored by Ventura Associates, 1211 Avenue of the Americas, New York, NY 10036 and presented by independent businesses. Employees of these, their advertising agencies and promotional companies involved in this promotion, and their immediate families, agents, successors, and assignees shall be ineligible to participate in the promotion and shall not be eligible for any prizes covered herein. SWP 3/95